I0653728

THE EUROPA EFFECT

COPYRIGHT DISCLAIMER

Parchman's Press, *Publisher since 2013*

Copyright © 2017 by Mengel, A.L.

All Rights Reserved. This book, or parts therof, may not be reproduced without permission of the publisher. Mengel, A.L. – © 2017 PP/AL

Cover Design by Shoutlines Design. Boston, MA, United States of America. Title Page(s) by Shoutlines Design.

Author Photo Rudicil Photography, Des Moines, IA, United States of America.

Published by Parchman's Press, United States of America.

1 2 3 4 5 6 7 8 9 10 || 10 9 8 7 6 5 4 3 2 1

All rights reserved. All plot elements originally created by author. Any similarity to any other work in any format, written or filmed, published or released; unpublished, unproduced or unreleased, is purely coincidental and unintentional. All elements of this book, for the purpose of storytelling, are fictional. All characters are originally created by A.L. Mengel. Any similarities to any person, living or deceased, is also unintentional and purely coincidental. Any similarities to any other fictional character, from filmed, published or unpublished work is unintentional and coincidental. Review quotes printed with permission. Research sources for Glossary based on multiple widely available sources of generally accepted scientific theory.

Film and Television interests should contact Parchman's Press, the author or designated representatives. This novel was published in the United States of America by Parchman's Press, printed by Createspace and distributed worldwide.

ISBN-10: 0-9963269-6-0 | ISBN-13: 978-0-9963269-6-4

REVIEWS

THE WANDERING STAR

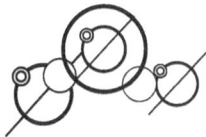

"Sad to see the last page come...captures the imagination...hang on tight for this one...Sci-Fi fans rejoice, this book's for you!" *- Jeremy Croston, Author "The Negative Man" series (via Goodreads)*

"Fascinating and Unusual Science Fiction to Love...a book you don't want to miss!" – via *Amazon*

"Fantastically cosmic and thought-provoking...the story is rich, robust, detailed...clearly for the sophisticated, thinking reader." – via *Barnes and Noble*

"We make our world significant with the courage of our questions and by the depth of our answers."

– CARL SAGAN

A.L. MENGEL'S BOOKSHELF

Ashes

The Quest for Immortality

The Blood Decanter

War Angel

The Wandering Star

#Writestorm

Curtains and Fan Blades

The Other Side of the Door

A NOTE FROM THE AUTHOR

BELOVED FRIENDS of 'The Writing Studio',

Like many young boys and girls growing up, I have always held a deep fascination with the cosmos. I think that's why I initially sat down to write *The Wandering Star*. That book will always hold a special place in my heart, being the "little story that could". It started as a writing exercise; I sat down to write a Science Fiction short story, and over the following weeks, it ballooned into a novel.

And then a series.

With the sequel, *The Europa Effect*, I was presented with new challenges in my writing. I envisioned a novel which would be set deep in the cosmos – featuring our own home "Milky Way" galaxy, among others. And I wanted to be as realistic as possible with the storytelling – set against backdrops that readers might have studied themselves.

The Europa Effect was conceived in mid-2016, shortly after the first novel of "The Vega Chronicles", *The Wandering Star*, went into print. When I had written *The Wandering Star*, I didn't want to make it too long of a novel, so I consider it a "short" sci-fi novel, although it's still a significant novel at 350 pages. Still, that story ended rather abruptly, and I knew that the story was destined to continue.

Primary research on *The Europa Effect* began in summer of 2016. It started with revisiting much of the same research that had been conducted for *The Wandering Star*, but also reading the works of Carl Sagan (*Cosmos, Contact*) as well as studying publically available NASA documents for space missions (Cassini, Voyager, Juno, among others).

In addition, this novel required the study of interstellar space travel (and methods as to how it can be achieved) as well as worm holes, black holes and cryogenic hibernation.

There is a short glossary of terms following this message which the characters use throughout the story. It's not entirely necessary to study to glossary – it's optional, as the characters do explain the process in various scenes – however reading through the glossary and its terms will educate readers to a degree (perhaps) enriching the story just a bit more.

GLOSSARY OF TERMS

ANTIGRAVITY – A force by which a body of positive mass would repel a body of negative mass.

ICEQUAKES – A phenomenon of Jupiter's ice-covered Moon 'Europa' where the tectonically linked plates shift and quake, similar to earthquakes.

EDL (Entry Descent Landing) – The NASA process of entering a planet's "atmosphere" and landing on unexplored terrain. For example, the Mars EDL is 7 minutes from 1) Entry into the upper atmosphere; 2) descent down towards the planetary surface; 3) landing on the Martian terrain. The EDL will vary based on the planet/moon and launch pod.

HEAT SHIELD – Protective shield for landing pods from atmospheric entry, where temperatures can exceed 1600 degrees.

MAGNETOSPHERE – The magnetic field around the gas-giant Jupiter, which is reported to reach millions of miles from the planet itself, outwards towards the sun. The magnetic field of Jupiter is extreme.

CRYOBOTS – Long, cylindrical "tubes" which [in theory] would be launched to the planetary surface ice to melt it. They are long, about the size of a telephone pole.

CRYOGENIC HIBERNATION – The process for interstellar space travel where the human body is cooled and hypothermia is induced for long periods of deep sleep.

SUPERMASSIVE BLACK HOLE – The largest type of black hole. A collapsed star with a huge and powerful gravitational pull. Once approaching the 'event horizon' escape from the "falling" is not thought to be possible.

EVENT HORIZON – The ring surrounding a black hole; it's the "point of no return" when attempting to escape its clutches.

ICE MOON – A nickname given to Jupiter's moon "Europa". The moon experiences temperatures of -220 degrees Celsius and is covered by a thick layer of ice. Mankind believes that there may be an undersurface ocean which might contain life.

WORM HOLE – A wormhole is a theoretical passage through space-time that could create shortcuts for intergalactic journeys across the universe.

SPACE-TIME – Any mathematical model that combines space and time into a single theory. They are purported to be related.

THE EUROPA EFFECT

PROEM

WE HAVE IGNITION

THE EUROPA EFFECT

A NOVEL BY A.L. MENGEL

THE
VEGA
CHRONICLES

FOR TY

The one who I can always count on, and who I would most want by my side on a cosmic voyage towards the unknown…

AND FOR SONG

You now soar through the Heavens; reveling in the cosmos, on your new, intergalactic journey. Miss you terribly. Say Hello to Mehki for me.

PROEM

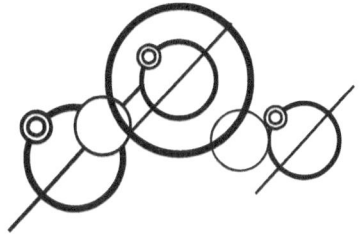

THE STUDY OF THE COSMOLOGY of the Universe had been overlooked in the latter days of the planet. It was when the days on the Earth had turned away from the exploration of the distant and the interstellar; and on the planet, the appreciation of music, and of art, and of philosophy, had waned.

It was during those years when there had been a transformation of such. A transformation of the human minds; but also, physically, of the planet; not only in the geology and the geography of the world, but also a change in the thought process of the people who populated the planet. Their beliefs, motives, and culture.

The long period of the shift had continued for generations…the subtle changes were initially ignored. But over the years, and as the generations progressed, the planet gradually re-terraformed itself. The period of the shift, which had been considered "long" based on the percentage of a typical human life, was insignificant on a cosmic scale.

And that period had become a quest for survival.

After the period of what became known across the planet as the *Great Shift*, those who remained had been labeled "the survivors" and those who perished were remembered. And the world changed drastically in the generations that followed.

During those years, man rarely looked up towards the Heavens. Those times on Earth had become a period of survival, and the thoughts of the cosmos were forgotten.

Until the day when a man had arrived unexpectedly to a colony known simply as "Sector B". He had been disheveled and dirty, physically near death as he had staggered towards the colony's outer doors. Those who had witnessed his approach recalled watching his silhouette against searing sunlight, which had cast radiation on the planet in those days. The man, the scout, had collapsed on arrival, seemingly near death. The colonists risked exposure and rushed to his side, saw that he was still living, and had him taken to medical. Over the following weeks he was nursed back to health, and was known through the colony population as 'the scout'.

Rumors traveled through the colony about what the scout's purpose was.

And when the scout was well enough to speak with them, the people of the planet were urged to look up towards the sky once again: for there was a message.

There was a beacon of hope; of light.

There were those who claimed they had seen a star; and also rumors of those who were thought to have spoken to a mystical star with a message.

And the message was survival.

They believed that the human race could live on, if they looked upwards and outwards. Their destiny was not to remain living underground with dwindling rations, heading toward extinction.

It was to journey outwards.

To reach beyond.

To trust, and to take a leap of faith.

But the aura of the planet had indeed changed. Culture had vanished; no longer were there orchestral performances in city centers; many artistic masterpieces were lost forever under the sea in cities that had been swallowed by oceans.

And it was then, quite unexpectedly, that the people of the planet had the visitor. It was he who was called the "scout". After the colonists spoke with him, he was regarded as a messenger of sorts.

But not everyone trusted the mysterious man. Some thought he had been a warrior, or perhaps a pirate.

But there were others who did trust him.

And even others still who thought he could be a 'messiah'.

But he had a message to deliver, and that was his purpose.

People were given the free will to choose to accompany him, or stay behind. But those who chose to stay behind, he had claimed, would experience a fiery death as the planet was destined to perish.

After the scout had come, after the people looked up towards the stars, and after the people's journey, there had been a feeling of despair that washed over those who waited for what was to come next.

For the journey that the people took had been a quest for survival. Leaving the safety of Sector B, out into an increasingly hostile, now foreign world.

The people, though, learned to trust the scout.

They followed him as he led them to salvation.

The masses of people found themselves standing in the midst of a large, sandy desert, on a planet which had become dangerous and uninhabitable. Radiation threatened from above during six months of sunlight. It had only been safe to venture out during the six months of darkness.

Half the world was flooded, and the other half was a barren desert. Forests and agriculture had slowly died off after the physical transformation of the planet took place once the rotation had slowed to a stop.

But the scout brought the people hope.

As they stood exposed to cosmic rays in a large desert clearing, underneath a rapidly lightening sky, they felt a twinge of the unknown. Dusty, sandy hills rolled along the plains around them towards the horizon. The sky was starting to turn from black to dark blue.

But they still felt safe, at least to a degree. For they didn't quite remember much before seeing the massive, dark cylinder in the sky that hovered over the dry and dusty landscape. As they looked up at the dark hovering spacecraft, the rest of the thoughts of the dying planet gradually faded away.

It was a massive ship; one that was miles long and wide, one that would travel vast distances at speeds that mankind had never been able to achieve.

She stood and looked up at the gargantuan, dark structure which hovered in the pre-dawn sky. It looked like an immense, hovering silhouette, as the sky became lighter behind it. The cylindrical ship was like nothing mankind had ever seen before: it levitated above the surface of the planet, and stretched for miles, causing a shadow in the fading darkness of the sands.

The sun was about to rise.

But the planet, the Earth, had not rotated; it had not experienced its twenty-four hour day in many years. Man had science and knowledge, but the specific reason why the planet ceased to rotate remained a mystery. Newscasts, over the generations, had many scientific experts discussing the matter; theories abounded. But no one really knew *why* things happened the way they did.

The sun, as it approached with its light, was no longer thought of a friend…but rather a foe. For the atmosphere changed, along with the topography, and the ozone layer – and its protection – faded.

The weakened troposphere caused radiation concerns during daylight months, and the phenomenon only slightly abated during the months of darkness.

For during the period when the Earth's rotation slowed, and the topography of the planet changed, society and culture crumbled; it devolved into underground societies of those who had nearly forgotten the world above; the cities were reduced to skeletons, overgrown and partially reclaimed by nature. The once thriving cities had been abandoned. The emerging cultures of the underground had different levels of civility; others were simply uncivilized.

But she remembered her own group as being quite orderly and sophisticated.

Sector B had been the name of her organization. It had been built in the years when those on the planet discussed the *Great Shift*.

But it was reported to be one of the most technologically advanced underground cities in existence. Many of the inhabitants were philosophers, scientists, engineers, theologians. And a result, they were one of the most scientifically knowledgeable underground societies, if not the most.

Located in the dry sands underneath the skeleton of abandoned skyscrapers of what had once been known as Miami, construction began on Sector B once news of the shift had been confirmed and the evacuations commenced.

But, she remembered, at Sector B, they had been just as skeptical as the others when the scout had arrived.

As she stood in the imposing shadow of a ship which they had been led to, a ship which had not been built on Earthly soil; a ship which the survivors had been told would be the ultimate leap of faith; the ultimate mystery, and take them to the even more mysterious.

But she had never thought that her life would amount to this: to a period of total and utter dependence; on a quest for her survival, standing in sands that she would no longer see, or feel between her toes.

She looked down towards her feet.

Her boots were caked with the mud from the journey, and the logo from ROVER 1 was almost completely covered in the dark, wet sand. She closed her eyes as a single, solitary tear streamed down her cheek.

Her face showed experience.

The ridges on her cheeks caused the tear to fall erratically, but its destination was always the same place: the corner of her thin lips.

She wiped it away, raised her head and opened her eyes.

The sky was warming and the horizon was lightening. The sand was no longer dark and dirty but a light brown as the sky brightened in minutes.

The shadow the ship cast had been cool and comforting in the lightening sky; and the people huddled in the inviting darkness. There were several others in stark white uniforms; they appeared to be the ones in command, but she did not know their origin. They looked human. But they could not have been. Had the eternal question been answered?

It appeared so.

When she thought of the scout who had arrived at Sector B so unexpectedly, thoughts of a cosmic origin entered her mind.

But as they dashed through the crowds, barking orders to get inside, bringing the people who stood in queue throughout the sand leading up to the ship to ignore the lines and seek shelter, they seemed all too…human.

All too familiar.

"Seek shelter now!" one of those in white commanded. "Avoid the sunlight!" A group of those in white filed down the deck, and turned towards the outer planks.

She watched them. They truly looked the same as the people of Earth.

Exactly the same.

Had they not been dressed completely in white, she would not have been able to tell that they hadn't been survivors, but actually had arrived with the ship.

There was not any difference, on the forefront, when she watched them gather the people who were waiting in the sands. She saw their sense of urgency.

For the sun was quite hostile in those days.

Once they had lived underneath the grounds of dusty, abandoned equatorial cities in a network catacombs; entire populations in dwellings that reached downwards into the crust, level by level accessed via elevators and stairs that descended deeper into the ground, in a clinical, stone environment with artificial sunlight, little heat, and an overall sense of despair.

She saw the lines of people waiting in cues to board; it appeared as if the colonies all were evacuated, as if the assault of the sun weren't so near.

The survivors were now standing, exposed, under the lightening sky and the fading stars…when they had been told, for their entire lives, to avoid the sunlight. And even though those in white raised their arms and their voices, the people were slow to move to the darkness of the unknown spacecraft that cast a gargantuan shadow across the sands; some fought those in white; some survivors ran back towards the sands, with wide eyes, falling backwards as they lost their footing.

But their loved ones looked on, their faces shifted in pain, tears streaming down their cheeks. They would call out to their son, or father, daughter or uncle, pleading with them to go in the shadow.

To get out of the sunlight.

That there was radiation and death in the harsh brightness.

And the sky continued to lighten.

Some looked over towards the giant, foreign ship as others retreated closer towards it and stood in its shadow.

The world was not what it once was.

Despite the amnesia felt by the population, of culture forgotten and economics lost, there was this one woman who watched the scene play out before her; she saw those in white act as protectors of her people.

And this one solitary leader, who had remembered a world that once was, observed what it had degraded to as they stood in line waiting to board.

Her hair, the color of crimson, blew across her face, as she brushed it aside, watched the people in white work frantically to shepherd the remaining survivors towards the ship.

Those who stood in the sands were urged to get into the safety of the ship as the guards stood at the perimeter of the throngs of survivors, their arms outstretched.

One man in white, closest to the ship, looked out towards his other warriors, his hands balled into fists and resting on his hips. His face was crinkled in concentration, as he observed his workers in white.

They all stood, their arms outstretched, containing the survivors. The others, men and women, looked towards their leader, as he looked back at them, and as the winds picked up, blowing his hair back, he barked a command as the people in white took a step forward.

Several survivors lost their footing.

One woman screamed and shortly after a baby wailed.

Two men snapped around to a man in white. "She has fallen and she is with child!" one of them said. "Look at her baby!" Other survivors swarmed around the fallen woman and crying infant, as others looked up at the ship, eyes wide, their faces shifted in concern.

The woman waiting in line pulled some strands of her red hair away from her eyes.

She watched the scene play out as the line rushed forwards. She was now leaning on the railing of the deck, with others who had already cleared the medical tables and saw the remaining survivors resist.

She took a deep breath and held it.

She looked back at the terrain, and gasped as the sun peeked over the horizon. The faint dome of light; once a harbinger of warmth and life, now something to bring death and destruction?

"Get them inside!" she called out. But her voice could not penetrate the chaos.

She looked at the others in smaller cues in a line of tables with others who sat in chairs asking the approaching survivors medical questions, entering information in scanners, as others waited near the railings.

Had the ship arrived just in time? Was this their destiny as a human race?

To enter a rescue ship, with those who looked like them, but clearly *weren't* them, and trust them, implicitly and without reservation, and take the ultimate leap of faith?

And then she took a breath as a finger tapped her shoulder.

She turned around and looked behind her.

It was Jeremiah.

The light hit his face from the side, highlighting his close cropped hair, giving it a golden hue. The awkward angle of the light did nothing to age him as she felt it had to her over the years when the light would hit her face "a certain way". When the wrinkles would stand out, and the bags under her eyes would fall into a shadow. When she stood in the full light, she appeared far more youthful; more beautiful. But for Jeremiah, he was at the age when the light did not yet matter. His cheeks were full, but not chubby, rather youthful and athletic. She had always thought he had a nice bone structure.

His eyes were vibrant and bright, and his teeth white and straight. His clothes hugged his chest. He had always been fit. She'd remembered that from Sector B. Jeremiah had been the one who would always be the first to volunteer for physically demanding tasks, and she always thought that he was younger than he actually was. She remembered watching him skip through the hallways in a half-walk-half-run, dashing towards whatever the problem was at the time. She also remembered sitting with him in the dining hall, on multiple occasions, as he laughed with his brilliant teeth, running his hands though dirty blonde hair as he shuffled from foot to foot and told her about the daily tasks and his love for botany.

He approached her and smiled a tired smile. There was a smudge of dirt on his cheek and he was unshaven.

She could smell his sweat, but it wasn't pungent nor offensive. But he had a certain scent about him, as none of them had bathed for days.

She looked him up and down. He was still quite dirty from the journey across a dry, dusty terrain.

"Counselor Abagail," he said. "Look out there. Do you see that?" He pointed towards the horizon. The sky was pale, but not fully bright. The rolling sandy desert hills reflected the newborn morning light. They were nestled under the shade of the awning covering the check-in tables. But outwards, over the sandy landscape, the people scurried towards the receiving area like ants, with the people in white ushering them closer to the medical receiving tables.

As the survivors approached the hull, they fought for access to a small walkway; a ramp that was only wide enough for a single person.

Counselor Abagail approached the railing and looked out at the sandscape.

Her mouth dropped open.

"What…"

"Is that from the sun?" Jeremiah asked, leaning in closer towards her, placing his hands on the metal railing.

She turned her head as she watched the rays pierce into the ground; a brilliant wall of light penetrating into the sands. The people who had stood in line scattered towards the ship. Several other officers dressed in grey uniforms rushed towards the edge of a long, black railing which boarded the edge of the receiving area.

A tall man dressed in a fitted white uniform stood at the edge of the walkway with his hands on his hips. His face was stern and shifted. "Open the gate! Get them to quarantine!" Several more officers in similar white dress approached from the northern side of the deck as a hydraulic gate opened on the far wall with a hiss and a thud.

Another officer stood at the end of a long ramp as the gates snapped open. "Go inside the hydraulic doors! Get them into the receiving chamber!" His voice boomed as the people spilled up towards the ship.

Hundreds, possibly thousands of people, who had stood in queue for hours, ran from the sandy clearing below, trampling each other. Counselor Abagail looked out at the sunray and watched it penetrate the ground and move closer to them. She nudged Jeremiah who was fixated on the ray. "Is that what I think it is?"

"It's penetrated the troposphere!" he said. "This is what happens when the sun becomes hostile! We must go with them! Now, Abby!"

She looked out at the sands as the light filtered towards the ground, exploding a wall of sand towards the ship. It rained down on the people on the walkway, who huddled down towards the floor.

"It looks like grenades are going off!" she said, as Jeremiah pulled her arm, dragging her towards the doors. Dirt shot into the air a plume of light reached the landscape. "Let's get inside, Abby! We don't have much time before that ray moves right over us!"

The guards rushed the sea of people inwards, through the expansive hydraulic doors. As the people filed inside, they gathered in a large receiving chamber, with a soaring ceiling. Counselor Abagail and Jeremiah stood in the masses of people. The medical personnel who had lined the exterior docks carried their tables inside as the doors hissed, lowered and closed with a deep, resonating thud.

"It's radiation!" Someone screamed as the tables were placed against a far wall.

"It's already too late!" Another phantom voice was heard through the bedlam. As the people huddled inside a large receiving chamber, several doors further down the chamber lowered with a hiss.

Deep thuds shook the metal floors as the guards walked the edge of the chamber. Counselor Abagail leaned against a nearby wall, closed her eyes and bent over, placing her hands on her knees, and caught her breath. "Jeremiah?"

"I'm here," he said, stooping down next to her. She looked up and over at him, panting, and shook her head.

They could barely hear one another over the chorus of voices resonating through the crowds in the vast chamber.

"What was that Jeremiah?"

He leaned his head back on the wall. "Cosmic radiation. That'd be my guess."

She gasped. "Have we been exposed?"

Jeremiah shook his head. "Hopefully not, but won't know unless radiation sickness occurs."

She remembered the news reports before the *Great Shift* had happened. Before the days at Sector B, when she had been standing in her tiny living room. She had held a small battery operated television in her hands, for the lights had already gone dark. *Radiation reaching life threatening levels,* the news anchors had warned.

"Good God…so it's really happening. Everything that they said? What they predicted?"

"It's already happened, Abby. The radiation is real. Back in Sector B, we never saw this, did we?"

"We were living underground."

"Exactly," he said.

She shook her head slowly, as she watched the scene play out before them.

Her mouth dropped open as she looked out at the people, standing in the middle of the expansive receiving chamber, some sitting on the cold, hard steel floor, others sitting on bags and backpacks. "And now we have no other solution but this?" She turned around and saw Jeremiah looking out at the people, nodding.

Jeremiah broke his stare and turned to her. "It appears so. The scout may very have been right. The troposphere is failing, Abby."

She straightened herself and looked back over at the people. It was bedlam. People speaking over others, but nothing was discernable. Babies were wailing over the chaos. Women were disheveled and dirty; men were approaching guards and demanding answers.

Had they been the fortunate ones?

"Jeremiah, where are the rest of the people from Sector B? No one looks familiar."

He stood up and looked out at the sea of people, huddled in the expansive receiving chamber. "I can't see anyone directly. I'm sure they're here, Abby."

"But now we're on this ship. Locked in. What if they are still outside?"

Jeremiah shook his head. "Then they are probably dead, Abby."

She gasped.

He put his arms around her and shook his head. "No, no Abby. They boarded with us. I'm certain they have. We just need to find them. But I'm sure they boarded when we did. Don't you remember?"

She shook her head. "I can't remember. Everything seems hazy…everything beyond this ship. Like a blur."

She raised her head from his shoulder and looked over towards the hydraulic doors. There were small, rectangular windows a short distance from the crest of the ceiling. Faint light shined through.

"I…" she said. She closed her eyes and shook her head. "I honestly can't remember. We boarded…and then the ray came…it was all so sudden. So chaotic."

"But now, here we are, safe and sound on the ship."

"I'm just having a hard time remembering…"

Jeremiah squeezed her shoulder gently. "Look up there."

A small opening, about the size of a door, appeared as a section of the wall raised to a rectangle of darkness behind the platform. The small ledge was surrounded by a railing and extended outwards from the wall as several other officers in white dress uniform on a platform which elevated outwards above the people.

"Let's listen," Jeremiah said. "I think they are about to address us..."

I have called on you to be a leader. —

The Wandering Star

6

THE RED OUTPOST

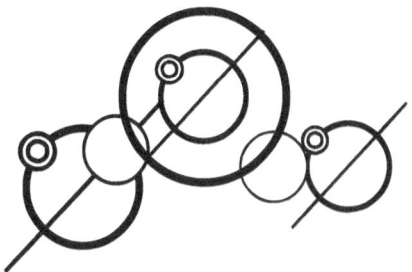

COUNSELOR ABAGAIL opened her eyes. All she saw was darkness. Her vision was blurred to black, and she felt a heaviness about her.

She was wearing something.

Something heavy over her clothes. It was dark inside, and she could move about. But she was too weak to lift her limbs. And when she tried, she felt the bulky over suit.

And as her eyes adjusted, she started to see what was surrounding her and wondered where she was. Fleeting thoughts penetrated her mind. Tiny glimpses of cosmic scenes; of colorful palettes which seemed interstellar in nature, but she could not recall their origin.

She was surrounded by darkness; but there still was a degree of sight.

She moved her eyes to her left. It was too tight to move her neck very much. Whatever she was wearing seemed to be mildly constrictive.

She saw three small screens to the left of a rectangular window in the front of her vision sight, but it was clouded. She wasn't sure what it was – it could have been a visor or faceplate. As her eyesight continued to improve, the rectangular visor appeared blurred and sandy, but some faint light filtered in; she was still unable to see through it; it was like trying to look through a layer of waxed paper. But it certainly felt as though she were wearing a heavy, dark suit.

She could hear the howl of winds; and noted that the winds did not penetrate the heavy, protective apparatus. Her mind continued to clear and she attempted to move again.

Her body felt small inside the vast space inside the suit.

Several colorful lights illuminated.

Something seemed to wake up.

The large, heavy helmet weighed on her head, which took effort to hold upwards and steady, and her vision was nearly dark save the brightly colored LED screens which displayed data of her health (heart rate, pulse, blood pressure) as well as several other names listed in a column down the opposite side (Winston, Jeremiah, Eli, Nelson) with a small rectangle to the left of each name displaying fuzzy, black and white static.

As she regained energy, she slowly reached her hand around to her visor and wiped it clear.

Dust.

Dirt, but a deep red tint.

The shadows of rocks which peppered themselves through the sand in the orange hue of the foreground, reached outwards towards the horizon.

The view from her helmet assembly was what she had expected before initial landing – a harsh, red, sandy environment; mountains and orange sands as far as the eye could see, soaring outwards towards the horizon. The relentless winds blew sand clouds with the force of a hurricane under an orange tinted sky.

Her temples pulsed as she closed her eyes, tightly, and opened them again. The same blur in her vision hadn't yet cleared. She had felt there was a twinge of something cosmic; as she closed her eyes, she could see a vast, black ocean filled with an immeasurable array of tiny, white stars, and then a burst of colorful gases, soaring past. In the midst of her mind's vision, of her dream, or her memory. When she opened them, she saw what had been the reality before her, at least she so thought. But when she closed her eyes again, she saw the star scape paint its way across her mind.

Had there been a certain period of travel, of interstellar movement, that she could only struggle to remember? There had not been a period of amnesia, had there?

Her mind was fuzzy as she felt that she had just awoken. The fuzziness remained, like the haze blanketing the pale sky above her. There had not been a distant journey of galaxy jumping; this red surface seemed familiar. She had recognized it from the photos of her youth. She must have. She hadn't remembered anything before the dust storm. But now it seemed the dust had cleared. There was no blowing red sand in across her helmet.

But there had been something that was indescribably different: for a habitable zone seemed foreign; the dust vastly different than snippets of windstorms that penetrated her mind.

It was not Earth.

That was something that she could remember; that she could fathom. There was a certainty about her distance from where she believed that she had originated from; but the memories were just small snippets. More tiny pictures flashing through her mind, scenes of a distant world, a place that despite its far reaches from her, it felt, somehow, familiar.

She was jolted back to the present as a whippet of dust blew on her faceplate and concealed her vision.

She brushed her hand over the thick plastic, wiping a messy vision: the winds were increasing; jolting bursts but not constant.

And she was not standing.

She was still lying on the ground.

And as she struggled to see through the blowing dust, she saw the light metal glisten through the blowing clouds.

She knew.

The thought penetrated her mind, like an arrow shot square into the center of her head. There was some familiarity to the photos she had remembered studying as a little girl; for she recognized them in a flurry of revelation: it was the angry red planet. The cousin, the neighbor.

The sun had not risen on Mars, but there was light somewhere.

Yes. That was it. She was on Mars.

Her mind did not allow her to see beyond the revelation; the familiar became real as the winds increased with ferocity. But there was a blank space. A chalkboard wiped clean; a distant memory that was floating through another galaxy which she could scarcely retrieve.

She struggled to move but the suit was far too heavy.

It was as if she were lying under a mountain of boulders; but she was not. The winds increased without warning as she felt the pressure of the sand and dust against her limbs; but she lay close to the ground as she saw in the corner of her viewfinder: the winds had increased; there was a storm approaching.

She held her arms over her face to cover from the force of the sudden winds instinctively, though the glass was rated for Mars windstorms.

She had thought that voices surrounded her, but all she heard on COM 1 was static. "Jere! Jere, where are you?!"

But there had been no answer.

She hoisted herself up.

She turned her back to the assault of the winds and cupped her hands around her eyes. She looked back towards the ROVER, its muted gleam was scarcely visible through the blowing sands.

Had the team still been there?

She noted the heaviness on her back and reached around.

She was still carrying the small, sandy backpack. Yes. She remembered that tiny detail.

She struggled to lift her feet. She grimaced, mustered her energy and trudged forward. "Jere!" she called out. His LCD panel was still blank. No response. Just the howl of the winds. "Winston! Eli? Are you guys still there?!"

She had called each of the names listed on the side column of her helmet control panel, but there was no answer.

Thunder crashed overhead as light flashed around her. She looked up towards the sky. The clouds appeared just as red tinted as the terrain. Certainly it would not rain, would it? And if it did, what would the rain consist of?

The winds abated and she saw the dark silhouette of the ROVER ahead.

Could be fifty or a hundred yards, but probably no more.

The winds and the sand had concealed it. But her vision had been so clouded. She looked up. There appeared to be a reddish tint to the sky.

No view of the sun.

Had they made it back to camp?

She trudged forward, towards the ROVER, taking each step with a wincing effort. She could feel the perspiration on her forehead just before the suit cooling mechanism engaged.

As she approached, a deep rumble emanated from the sandy ground as she stumbled and fell against the hard metal.

She looked down at the ROVER.

But it wasn't like the ROVER she had remembered back on Earth. It was a similar vehicle. Large, with three rugged wheels along the side. Made of different metals and a new design, there was something quite foreign about this model.

She flopped around on her back, leaning on the side of the ROVER.

The sky appeared red.

More of a pastel; sand blew in giant, roaming dust clouds on a cloudless day. The sun was visible, she could see, as she raised her arms and shielded her eyes. As she peered up and towards the shining star, it was filtered; dulled, and cast a gray hue.

"Jere! Winston! Eli?"

Where had the team gone? She fought the door of ROVER open and fell inside, hoisting herself onto a seat, struggling under the weight of the suit. She reached over and slammed the door once her legs were on the floor. The winds were now muffled, and she looked ahead.

There was certainly something different about her location. She could see the Martian terrain through the front dashboard.

It was not the Earth which she remembered.

It was not the same ROVER either. She reached out and touched the buttons, lightly running her gloved fingertips along the red and blue buttons. She raised her head and looked ahead.

Swirling dark clouds moved overhead, racing across the sky. She pointed up towards the red sky. "Are those dust clouds?" Her voice cracked and sounded broken and muted inside her helmet.

But there was movement on the horizon that caught her eye. She did a double take and looked again, studying the ferocity of the winds.

She looked intently.

A crinkle formed in the center of her forehead as she watched the terrain for movement.

In the center of her visor, through the window of the dash, she saw a figure; something dark, blotchy. It could have been pulsating.

Or alive.

A shadowy figure.

Difficult to discern from the distance. Her vision was muted by blowing dust, and fading light. She looked up and saw the sun in the distant Martian sky – fiery yet faded, muted but still penetrating the clouds.

Through the dust clouds, she looked back down and saw the shadowy figure moving slowly across the horizon; a large, dark figure, an unclear shape, but the distance was great.

Her breathing was slow and shallow and then she caught her breath. "Jere! Come in! Is that you out there? Someone from our team?" She smashed her palm against the small, black screen on her forearm.

C.A. REPORTING. LOCATION?

She lumbered out of the ROVER, hoisting herself onto the sand and stood up.

She moved forward, and winced at the heaviness of her suit.

As the winds tore against the horizon, as the dust covered her visor, she reached up and wiped it away again.

Her strength appeared to be gradually returning, and walking started to become easier, but still took considerable effort.

She focused on the shadow ahead.

She held steady, standing against the assault of the sandy winds, watching the dark figure; studying it, intently, without distraction. Even the sand which gathered on her visor was wiped away with her hand, which she had not noticed.

For all she saw was the dark figure.

She took a short, quick breath.

Had it moved?

She reached up and wiped her visor again.

There was a mindless feel to the situation.

She did not recognize the commands her mind was sending to her body; but she did not act in surprise or shock when her right foot lifted from the ground, heavy it was, the weight of the suit contributed to the great effort of taking a step.

But she moved forward, slowly.

She struggled against the increasing winds, and despite the reaction of lowering her torso towards the ground, and leaning forward, walking into the fierce winds, she remained upright, focused on the dark figure. She wiped her visor again and looked ahead. It was a large blotch across the auburn sky, just at the horizon where it met the terrain; it was flat on either side. The darkness rose upwards, at an angle, reaching inwards and upwards towards the sky.

And then she felt herself moving again.

Slow, determined steps, the same heaviness in each leg. She broke her stare and looked down at the keypad on her arm. She paused for a moment and started typing.

JERE. COME IN? STRANGE DARK
FIGURE AHEAD. GOING TO
EXPLORE.

She looked back up and proceeded ahead not expecting an answer. Until there was a tiny beep in her ear, scarcely audible against the roar of the winds.

In the dark interior of her helmet, a small screen glowed to the left.

In the three small squares that had been only random electronic noise, one of them changed to black. But it was not a deep black as if the monitor had turned off, but rather a black screen, as if it were attempting transmission. And then she gasped as the words flashed on the screen:

INCOMING MESSAGE.

She gasped.

She stopped walking looked down at her forearm. Next to the keypad were three green buttons. She pressed the left button and typed on the keypad.

JEREMIAH? ARE YOU ALIVE?

The screen flashed and cut back to noise.

She reached around and smacked her helmet. The screen cut back to black and then another flash; a scene, just for a fleeting moment, of the ground.

She smacked the side of her helmet again.

The screen flashed again, and then the image held steady.

The ground was at an angle, on the right side of the screen. The helmet was lying on its side.

And it was most certainly Jeremiah's cam, according to the listing on the right column. He had to have been lying on his side. And the camera was working. She tripped over a rock and fell to her knees as she reached up and pounded on the left green button. Her hands shook as she typed.

LOCATION? I WILL COME TO YOU.
SEND LOCATION!

The screen flashed to black once more, and then the image returned and held steady. It was at a slightly different angle; there was a dark blotch in the right corner.

And then she gasped and looked ahead at the dark figure nestled in the center of the terrain.

Could it have been where she was thinking it was?

HOLD POSITION. I AM COMING.

She wiped her visor and headed forward and ignored the heaviness of the exploration suit. Every few minutes, she reached up as she continued to wipe the sand from her visor, but did not break her stare at the dark figure.

She knew that it was much farther away that it had appeared, but the ROVER was far behind her; she was in an unknown location, alone, with no known transportation, no known rations.

No sense of where she was. Or how she got there. Or what had happened to her and her team.

She approached the shadow of the dark figure as the freak sandstorm abated.

The sunlight was still muted and grey, the sky covered in orange tinted clouds, but she could see better, and since the sands were no longer blowing, she did not have to reach up to wipe her visor any longer.

The dark figure had not been a figure at all.

It looked like a giant mountain, reaching upwards into the clouds. It cast a dark shadow on the terrain, standing in command. As she looked towards the base of the mountain, she saw a glimpse of silver, or perhaps steel. Was that another ROVER?

She ran forward, gasping at the weight, but determined. As she neared the base, she recognized the ROVER design from before. She could remember now. Her mind was functioning again. It was the same ROVER that they had traveled in when they first hit the surface of Mars. Somehow had Jeremiah taken another ROVER to explore this mountain?

The fog on her mind was lifting; she remembered very specific details: Jeremiah had been with her. So had Eli and Winston. And Moses.

They had been sent on a mission to reach the Red Outpost.

She even remembered the details of this new ROVER; her mind saw visions of the coordinates of the second ROVER on the illuminated screens on the front dash.

But despite the revelation, there still had been a gap: a necessary exclusion in her thoughts. And the scene that played out in front of her, as she reached the base of the dark mountain.

The suit, which lay on its side at the threshold of the mountain shadow, was facing away from her, looking towards the dark rocks. It looked brighter than the rest of the sand and rock.

She ran to the dirty white suit, which seemed to glow in the fading light.

Was it Jeremiah?

The suit was lying on its side, the visor pointed at an angle, away from her, looking towards the base of the rocks.

She fell to her knees and tapped her hand on the visor. "Jere!" She moved around to the other side and she gasped.

The helmet was empty.

She smashed her palms against the legs, and the material collapsed. She shook her head and fell back into a sitting position.

The helmet was still on the side, pointing towards the dark mountain, and she looked at the monitor, still showing the same view.

She hung her head down, closed her eyes, and felt the warmth of fresh tears running down her cheeks.

There hadn't been anyone.

There couldn't have been.

She sat, in a tiny area in the red sands of Mars, in the dark shadow of an unknown mountain, sheltered from the raging winds just feet away. But the suit, empty.

Lying in the sand in the shadows, its visor and camera pointing towards the mountain.

Do you want me to go there, Jeremiah? Is that where you are? Is your empty helmet pointing the way?

She turned her head to the left and looked in the across the base of the mountain. She couldn't tell with exactness in the dim sunlight, but she thought she saw a reflection in the center of the darkness.

A tiny beam of light reflecting back at her.

Could it be movement?

And then she looked back at the suit lying in the sand. The visor looking in that direction.

Are you showing me the way?

Her legs felt heavier than before.

And weaker.

As she struggled to get up, she almost lost her balance as she cocked her knees and slowly rose to a stand. She looked in the distance, as the reflection continued its call. The beam of light shined against her visor, and she turned her head away. Could something be so reflective in the dim light on the surface of Mars?

She trudged forward and looked down at the suit once again.

Where are you, Jeremiah?

It had certainly been his suit, no doubt. But where had he gone? The atmosphere was far too thin and toxic for humans to breathe. Had they set up a camp? Could he be there?

She shook her head in frustration and took a deep breath. There was no indication that she had come to Mars alone. And a huge memory gap. No matter how hard she tried, she still struggled with any memory concerning the specifics of her team.

Or how she got to the surface in the first place.

The reflection beamed in her face to near blinding effect as she arrived at the base of the mountain. She was deep in the shadows; the sand appeared black, dark grey in spots. But the reflection – brilliant, bright, white.

She waited several yards away and looked towards the side of the dark mountain.

It appeared to be its own source of light.

The sunlight was too thin and scarce this deep in the canyon. She turned and looked out towards the opening. The sky appeared lighter. The suit lay much further than she thought.

Had she really come that far?

And where were the other suits?

She looked back at the suit lying in the distance once more.

What are you trying to show me?

She shuffled forward, scanning the base of the mountain, turning her head to the left, and then over towards the right. She held her hands up across her visor as the light brightened; it emanated from a perfect rectangle in the midst of the dark mountain, like a star shining brightly, cosmic.

And then, towards the far right, she saw another shadow. A silhouette, something rising from the ground. She turned back towards the suit and looked at which direction the visor was pointing. She moved out of the beam of the light and headed towards the shadow.

Closer, and closer, until she stopped, fell to her knees, and hung her head. A flood of emotion washed over her, as she cried openly. There hadn't been a time when she had felt so alone. So distant from anything familiar.

So far away.

She held her breath for a moment and wished she could wipe the tears from her eyes. She knew, as her vision, wet and clouded, slowly cleared, that the mounds could only mean one thing.

Had she lost them?

Had she buried them?

And why couldn't she remember?

She sat, hanging her head down, next to the three mounds of dirt, wishing she had the answers.

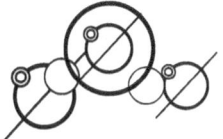

THERE WAS A CERTAIN VIEW of Mars.

The Red Planet.

The one that had been next to Earth for millions and perhaps – even billions – of years. In actuality, from the creation of the Milky Way Galaxy.

There were those who argued that Mars had once been teeming with life.

That water had flowed on the surface.

That oceans surrounded the land masses; and the argument persisted: where there is water, *there is life.*

But humans could not harness the mystery of the planet; they were unable to travel and explore beyond the first mission.

It had been named SALVATION.

And on the days on Earth when the mission was scheduled to launch, news of the mission – and the name SALVATION – had become common in households across the world.

Mars to be Investigated for Life the headlines screamed. Many First-World countries contributed to the cause; the exploration of a neighboring planet, and the contribution to expanding humanity beyond their single, solitary home planet had been appealing to scores of governments and civilian organizations.

But then came the *Great Shift*.

And the objective changed.

Whereas people had a genuine interest in exploring outwards, it had been halted.

And the aura of the planet changed to survival.

There was a difference in looking upwards to the cosmos when water was crashing through homes and businesses as people rushed from the waters around the world.

But there had been one more mission.

It was the mission that no one had talked about.

No one had heard about it.

The news was silenced.

But a launch took place.

And even though the SALVATION had already landed on Mars, the second, secret phase of the mission planted Earthly DNA in a secure location in an area dubbed as "The Red Outpost".

And no one on Earth had heard about it, until it was revealed many, many years later, on a rescue ship, on a mission to save humanity.

She exhaled as her eyelids fluttered open.

All she saw was darkness.

There was a temporary ripple in her vision, as if her eyes were adjusting to the darkness.

A square cutout was in the middle of the wall at the opposite end of the room. Perhaps a window? It was long, rectangular, and there was a small, black line that surrounded another panel which matched the cream color of the wall.

She pulled the sheets down and reached outwards, away from the bed she was lying in. She turned to the side and felt around the darkness, but there was just a stark, cold plastic table on the edge of the bed.

And silence.

The room was black as night, as quiet as a grave, and there was a slight, deep hum which she could not quite place, but appeared to be emanating from the floor.

It might have been still in the early morning, perhaps?

And the sun had yet to rise.

But what had happened last night?

She closed her eyes again as she pushed the covers down with her feet. She tried, but couldn't remember anything from the previous night. She couldn't even remember going to bed.

She swung her legs out and over the side of the bed and placed her feet on the floor. It felt like cold linoleum. She saw the shadow of what looked like a snake lamp on the bedside table. It came on, by itself, with a snap and light bathed the room.

It seemed skinny yet long, stark white, and there were matching drapes hanging on the far wall. Furnishings were plain and also white. She turned around and looked back down at the bed, there were sheets, a blanket.

All white.

Had she been injured?

Was this a hospital room?

She fumbled through the sheets.

And then lifted the blanket up. No remotes, no call buttons. No televisions. No beeping machines next to her bed.

Just a plain, stark white room, sparsely furnished.

She sat up and swung her legs over the side. There was no emotion. No feeling. No sense of wonder as to where she was or how she got there. Just the simple hum that emitted from the floor.

A slight drone.

Deep, methodical, yet smooth.

Like a distant cello playing a single, solitary note; a piece of music which deemed itself eternal, with no rest, no pause at the end of the stanza.

The floor felt stark and cold and her knees sodden.

As she stood, she wobbled a bit, bending forward and grasping her knees with her hands, and startled at the soft feel around her bone.

She steadied herself on the bedside table and saw a bag marked "Drainage".

Was there some significance to this plain room?

Some secret foundation?

She walked over to the window and parted the curtains.

She gasped as it opened to a sea of stars. Tiny, pinpoint white dots in a black, motionless sky.

Nothing more.

Just the silence of the cosmos.

And then there was a knock on the door.

Three quiet raps.

And then the patience of silence.

She turned her head. The door seemed far across the room. It was just as white as the rest of the room. There was a tiny peep hole in the center.

But she waited.

The room was long, which to her seemed undeniably vast, like the heavens on the other side of the hull; and the door was too far to explore or travel to.

Three more raps came again, breaking the silence.

And then a muffled female voice. "Counselor Abagail? Are you awake? It is nearly time for the group."

The group?

She took a step closer towards the door, and then took a second step, never taking her eyes off of it.

And that small peep hole.

As she approached the side of the room, she looked over and saw the mess of covers on the small bed; the shining lamp on the bedside table; the white, barren chairs.

"Are you coming, Counselor Abagail?"

She moved a few feet towards the door.

The small peephole seemed larger now. She thought she could see the shadow of someone standing in the middle of the circle. She leaned forward, but she could not see who was standing outside.

Just a shadow.

Bits and pieces.

The image was inverted and curved.

She turned around once again. Looked back at the stars. This had to be a hospital room. She had to have been injured. On a ship?

Maybe that could explain the amnesia.

She swung the door open, looked down and saw a petite, smiling olive-skinned woman; her black hair was tied behind her face neatly and wearing a pants suit that was as stark white as the room.

The woman smiled and spoke softly.

"Have you drained the fluid in your knees?"

She shifted her face. "I…"

The woman entered and nodded.

"I see. I understand. Sit on the bed and we will take care of it." The woman guided Counselor Abagail to the bed and ushered her to sit. The woman picked up a small bag from the small, plastic nightstand and opened the drawer with her free hand. There was a plastic container of wrapped needles in the front corner; she fished one out and held it out to Counselor Abagail who looked at it with a look of bewilderment.

"You must take care of this each time you wake," the woman said, looking directly in her eyes. She explained the importance of knee fluid drainage as she pressed the needle into the side Counselor Abagail's leg.

She winced as the sharp needle pierced her skin.

She watched the woman attach the bag and tubing to the needle with precision as her knees felt lighter. Blood tinged fluid slowly filled the clear, plastic bag. She looked up as the woman made eye contact with her and smiled.

She smiled back.

The woman's teeth were a brilliant white contrast against her olive skin and dark hair.

"So...I...am here for a long time? How long have I been here?"

The woman removed the bag, stood and nodded as she went over to the bathroom and snapped on a bright, florescent light. Counselor Abagail could hear fluid draining into water.

"Yes, you have been here," the woman said softly. "But each morning you ask me the same questions. And we go through the same routine. Especially with your knees. And we go over the same procedure."

"What is wrong with my knees?"

The woman returned and fished the needle from the side of her knee seamlessly and without pain, and wrapped the tubing around the filled bag. There was the striking smell of alcohol, just for a moment, as she cleaned the skin.

As she rose and placed the unused items on the nightstand, she looked at her directly in the eyes, and started to apply a small, white, cylindrical object to the wound.

It looked like it could be a writing utensil.

She held it close to the side of her knee as a pinpoint blue light circled around the spot. "We are taking care of you," she said. "We are seeing that you are nourished. And later, in group, we will continue to explore your mind. But we do seem like we have been spinning our wheels lately."

"So I do not remember anything? I have trouble with my mind?"

She stood and looked down at her. She nodded. "Yes. This is the same conversation we have each morning, Abagail. The same exact one. And I would imagine you also had the same dream."

Her face shifted as she leaned back. "The same...dream?"

The woman turned and pressed a small, dark panel on the wall, as a large section retracted and gathered some white folded clothes. She stood before Counselor Abagail, her hands clasped in front of her. "That will be more of what we explore in group today," she said. "Now please, Ms. Abagail. There are facilities in that room. I will wait for you just outside the bathroom door as you ready yourself. Your clothes are laid out for you on the dresser." She gestured to a small box across from the bed. "Please hurry, they are waiting for you."

Counselor Abagail emerged from the bathroom wrapped in a white robe and her head wrapped in a matching towel. The woman in white held some folded dark clothes up for her. "Put these on," she said.

There was an announcement on the public address system which sounded throughout the ship. Counselor Abagail looked up towards the ceiling as a tinny, female voice filled the room:

ALL PERSONNEL TO ORIENTATION
CHAMBER AT ONCE!

The woman in white packed up the syringes and placed them in the top dresser drawer. "We must go," she said. "That announcement is for you and the others."

She stood slowly, dressed completely in black. She tied her red hair back behind her head. "Which…others?"

The woman in white placed her hand gently on Counselor Abagail's back and ushered her out to a barren, stark white corridor. There were others shuffling through the hallway – women in white, other women in black, dressed exactly like she was.

ALL PERSONNEL TO ORIENTATION
CHAMBER AT ONCE!

The message repeated, again and again, as they hurried together down towards the other end of the ship. The corridor was lengthy, and after a rushed walk, they reached a station with several pods where others were gathered.

"We will catch the hover tram," she said. "Take it to Borderline. From there, it's a short walk from the station." Counselor Abagail looked at the others standing at the pods. They stood in groups in black and white clothes. Perhaps uniforms? Most were silent. A few others chatted quietly among themselves. And most were asking questions to those in white. After a few minutes, there was a hum, and a train, or perhaps a tram, appeared from a long, dark tube on the opposite end of the terminal. It stopped in front of those gathered at the pods with a slight hiss, but overall it was nearly silent. Doors opened outwards in front of each pod, as those in white ushered the others inside.

As the tram started moving, the woman in white leaned in towards her ear. "The ship is very large," she said. "It would take too long to walk to borderline, so we take the tram."

Counselor Abagail nodded and leaned her head against the cool glass, watching the ship pass before their eyes. The transport tube lined the edge of the ship.

Counselor Abagail looked to her left and her mouth dropped open. The hull of the ship was entirely clear; through it, she saw the vastness of the stars.

The tube reached across the entire span of the corridor offering a stark contrast of the plain white walls, flooring and doors, on one side. On the other side, the black vast galaxy.

She turned her head to the side and stared at the red sphere that hovered in close proximity to their ship; she ignored the message which sounded an additional time as she looked at the fiery red globe, covered in the orange terrains, mountains and moving clouds.

"Is that?" She turned towards the nurse who nodded.

"Yes," she said. "That is the basis of your current mission. You will be going there." She grabbed Counselor Abagail's arm and urged her ahead.

"We must not be late," she said. "Please, let's move forward."

"I am going there?" she asked. "To Mars?"

"All will be explained in the chamber," she said as the tram pulled to a stop. "We're at borderline," she said as the doors opened. They headed down another corridor. As they reached the atrium of the orientation chambers, there were people scurrying about. Their white uniforms matched the interior.

The woman in white pointed Counselor Abagail to a large set of doors, which opened to rising chairs, in a darkened amphitheater.

"Go join them," she said. "I will speak with you later in group."

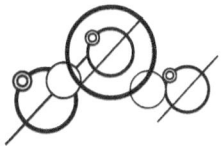

COUNSELOR ABAGAIL SLOWLY TURNED towards the doorway. Across the threshold, she saw the slant of the seats rising upwards. The entrance appeared to be mid-way up the rising seats, and when she paused on the verge of entering, she scanned the room.

As she looked up and to the left, and people filled the seats, a few were chatting among themselves quietly, but most were sitting, looking around the room with wide eyes. All were dressed in solid black, just as she was. As she paused for a moment, looking straight ahead, she focused on a man, a young brown-skinned man, sitting in a nearby seat, tapping his foot. He occasionally hooked his long bangs up and around his right ear, but it shortly fell just moments later.

And he would repeat the process.

He alternated between leaning forward, hunching over his knees, and then sitting back. He looked around the room nervously.

As she approached him, he looked up at her as she stood right next to his chair.

"Are you nervous?" she asked. She cracked a smile as she gestured to the empty chair. "Is that seat taken?"

He shook his head. "No, go ahead and sit."

For a few minutes, they sat next to each other in silence as they each watched the room with others who were in similar dress, who seemed equally confused and who slowly populated the seats. As Counselor Abagail studied the group of people, she looked over at the young man.

He was still fidgeting.

After a moment, he snapped his head towards her. "Yeah…you know why we're here?"

Counselor Abagail shook her head and sighed as she eased herself into the small, plastic chair. "Actually, I don't. I just woke up on this big ship. Don't remember anything else."

"Me too."

"I don't even know how I got here."

"Me neither. I woke up and this guy was in my room. All dressed in white. He said I had to drain my knees...I was like...am I in the hospital?"

"I don't think so, but I had the same thoughts. And I asked the same questions," she said. "But it seems to be a huge ship. Unless it's some sort of space station. But it feels like we're on a ship. Hovering. Or moving. Can't really tell."

"I don't get any of this," he said, looking forward and shaking his head back and forth. "I just find this all quite...strange."

Counselor Abagail chuckled softly. "I had the same thoughts. And a similar experience." She turned and faced the man, and extended her hand. "I'm sorry," she said. "Abagail. I've been called Counselor by the woman who helped me. But I'm not sure of the origin."

The man nodded as he shook her hand. "I'm a bit blurry myself. But at least I know my name!"

He smiled. "Eli DeJesus."

She nodded as she heard an audible tone sound from the ceiling.

All of the chairs which rose from a small, presentation area were now full of people. Everyone in deep black. Some wandered through the doors and quickly rushed to seats. Those had appeared to be among the last to arrive. She shrugged her shoulders and shook her head.

The tone sounded again.

A hush fell across the room as a small man wearing stark white appeared from a doorway just to the right of a presentation screen. He walked to a lectern in the center of the room and cleared his throat as Counselor Abagail raised her head and looked down at the lectern.

He appeared young, with dark hair.

"I have been sent by the Vegans, and I wanted to be clear why we have gathered you here," he said. He moved away from the lectern as he walked across the small presentation area, back and forth, as he spoke. "Like you, I am human. But those who I am working for are not."

There was a gasp from the audience.

The man nodded. "Do any of you remember how you got here?"

There was silence.

Counselor Abagail tried to remember. She remembered visions of what she thought had been the planet Mars, but before that, her mind drew a blank.

"My name is Moses. Nelson Moses. I have encountered and spoken with each and every one of you, although you may not remember it now. Now that we are millions of miles from your home planet."

Moses walked towards front row of seats, where a young man with close cropped hair had been sitting, watching him. Counselor Abagail watched Moses approach the man, look down at him, and smile. He then looked up at everyone. "Do any of you remember planet Earth?"

A blue sphere appeared above them, and levitated over the group. Heads turned upwards as Moses continued. "This planet had been your home for millennia. Many years you existed on this planet. Earth. The third planet from the sun. Covered mostly by water. In the goldilocks zone from your sun, at a perfect distance for habitation. Unlike other planets, either too close, and too hot, or too far away from the sun, and far too cold."

The hologram turned and they saw a single, giant land mass in the center. "They called that giant land mass *Pangea*. But, eventually, over millions of years, Pangea broke apart. The land mass split up, as large pieces of the land drifted apart, creating the oceans and continents you once knew, in some of your lifetimes. And others only know the more recent topography of the planet." As he spoke, the continents formed on the graphic.

He sighed, looking up at the hologram, his hands clasped behind his back, as the planet slowly stopped rotating. "And, as you see, this is what created your current predicament."

Counselor Abagail's mouth dropped open as she saw the water shifting, flooding the poles of Earth, as the planet again terraformed itself.

"We're not here today to explore the questions of why that happened to your planet," Moses said, returning to the lectern. "We are here today to address you directly. As I said before, I am a representative of the Vegans. But, like you, I am a human being."

A man a few rows up from the presentation area raised his hand as Moses nodded to him. The man stood. "Why Mars? Why are we at Mars? If we are looking to set up colony, hasn't it been determined in the past that Mars was a dead planet?"

Moses nodded. "Mars holds many mysteries," he said. "We are at a brief stop to obtain resources left at a research facility known as the Red Outpost. But Mars is not our destination."

Counselor Abagail stood. Moses looked up to her. "Yes, Abagail?"

She cleared her throat. "I need some explanation here. Because my mind is drawing a complete blank. I appear to be suffering from some version of short term memory loss." Some of the others spoke up, agreeing that they had the same condition.

"I only remember waking up today," she said. "A woman in white came into my room. She hooked me up to a drainage bag…what is happening?!"

The crowd swelled in agreement.

Moses raised his hands. "Please, everyone! Please. I must have your silence. I must have your attention."

Counselor Abagail called down to Moses. "How did we get here?"

The room quieted as Moses turned, walked back to the lectern, and raised his head to the blue hologram of the Earth, as it levitated, motionless above the group. "Look up there," he said.

Counselor Abagail sat down as Eli glanced over at her, his eyes wide. He shook his head slowly.

"Your planet has perished," he said as several gasps emanated from the room, which otherwise was under a hushed silence. "Or rather, it is dying."

"Your memories will return in time," he said. "But please understand. Amnesia is a side effect of the hypothermic fluids you have been administered for the journey. In order to preserve you as we travel through space, you will all be submerged in the liquid and ushered into a deep, hypothermic sleep."

Counselor Abagail looked over to her left and saw that Eli's eyes had widened. He leaned close to Counselor Abagail and whispered to her. "This seems familiar," he said. "Like we have done it before."

She nodded. "He said our memories would return. Maybe the liquid means something."

Moses continued: "A select few of you will be sent to the surface to collect the necessary items stored at the Red Outpost."

Eli raised his head and watched Moses.

The hovering planet above them now glowed red. "Mars?" he asked. He looked over at Counselor Abagail, who was intently listening. She made eye contact with him, and gestured towards Moses and Eli turned and listened again.

"*Utopia Planitia* is the destination area," he said, as the hologram turned and highlighted a large area on one side of the planet. "This is the area, as scientist theorized, that has the most propensity to contain life. There's running water there. And men set up camp there. That's the location of the Red Outpost."

The room remained quiet as the graphics changed. They zoomed inwards, as the rolling red sands of the Mars surface, outlined by rugged red rock terrain, filled the air above them. All eyes looked upwards and focused on the screen.

"Water runs beneath *Utopia Planitia*," he said, as the graphic zoomed further, through a surface crack, and bubbles and water splashed. "Life exists on that planet, which man had written off as dead."

The graphic zoomed out from the water and back to the surface, moving forward towards a small network of silver buildings. "The Red Outpost has been in place to ensure your survival," he said. "The survival of the human race. Everything is there that you need – DNA, seedlings, rare metals, elements…all you will need. And so this is a necessary stop for us in our journey."

A hand raised a few rows away from Counselor Abagail and Eli. Moses looked up and gestured to the man, who stood and introduced himself. "My name is Winston."

He turned and looked around the room, all eyes were focused on him.

"I, too, share the common problems with memory that you all describe. But I do remember some things which feel…at least to me…are from the distant past."

Moses nodded. "Such as?"

"I know I am from Africa. Nairobi. And I know I went to America before something that was called the 'shift'. But how I got here…how any of us got here…in space by Mars…is beyond my comprehension."

"Interesting," Moses said, nodding. "You have a different effect from the fluids. You remember much more."

Eli turned to Counselor Abagail once again. "He looks familiar too. I think we are supposed to know him."

She looked up and studied the man from Nairobi. She hadn't even heard of that city for years. But there was something about the name. Winston. Had she known him as well?

Moses called for the meeting to get back on track. "Of course each and every one of you will have different experiences and memories," he said. "Your memories, as I said, will return in time. And at different rates. You will not all react to the fluid in the same way."

The graphic disappeared as Moses shifted back towards the front row. "As I said, four of you have been preselected to take the mission to the Red Outpost. This has been based on historical data on you and the colonies that you inhabited back on Earth. And your skill sets. As for the rest of you, you will all be grouped off based on skill sets to form teams for the exploration and the remainder of our journey."

"What is that?" someone called out.

Moses nodded and smiled. "We are destined for the Jovian system. But more will be explained to you in the smaller sessions. We need to get all of you up to speed, and on the same page. So please, all of you, we will adjourn for breakfast, and all will be explained to you."

"What about the people in white?!" another man called out.

"All will be explained to you. This session has concluded. You will each be contacted individually for next assignment."

And Moses disappeared through a door on the far wall, as the amphitheater erupted in chatter.

Counselor Abagail sat back in the chair and watched the amphitheater break out in bedlam.

People stood and shouted, in a chorus of questions and confusion. Who were the people in white? What was their mission in the Jovian system? Who would be selected to journey to the surface of Mars?

She sighed and looked over at Eli, who sat next to her, as they didn't join the uprising. They sat together and Eli reached out, with his palm held upwards, and took her hand. She looked downwards, watching him; then she looked up, and saw his eyes. They were wide, inquisitive. He seemed so young. He was probably half her age. But there was something about him. Something that seemed so…familiar.

And then he took his other hand and placed it over their interlocking hands. "We are meant to be together," he said. "I can sense it."

She nodded and smiled as doors opened along the side stairs, leading from the lower levels towards the highest seats in the amphitheater.

There were those in white which appeared at each door in small groups.

When Counselor Abagail looked up, she recognized the smiling olive-skinned woman from earlier.

"Do you feel more informed?" she asked, never breaking her smile.

Counselor Abagail shook her head. "Not at all. But I did make a friend."

Her smile fell. "You must come with me now. Your group has been pre-determined and they will be waiting for you." She reached for Counselor Abagail's arm and ushered her out of the seat. "Come with me please," she said, as she led her amidst the crowds and back into the corridor.

The Breakfast Hall was located in the center of the ship.

Counselor Abagail was led by her woman dressed in white through the corridors towards the hover tram on the Borderline, just as Eli had been. She looked around the terminal. There were others dressed in black, just as she had been, paired with one dressed in white, just as she had been.

But she could not see Eli.

She sighed.

He seemed to be the only one who had any sort of familiarity in this increasingly unfamiliar world.

The tram pulled up with a hiss and the woman turned, made eye contact with Counselor Abagail, and ushered her towards the platform. "We must move quickly," she said. They entered the Borderline, and Counselor Abagail stood on the exterior wall of the tram as it accelerated along the side of the hull. She looked outwards, at the countless stars, and wished there had been more to the orientation. And who were the four who were to be chosen for the mission?

Several minutes later, the tram hissed to a stop at Central Station, at the midpoint of the ship.

The doors slid open to a chorus of activity: there were those dressed in white, others dressed in black, all were scurrying in many different directions.

There were shops.

Offices. Bars and restaurants. She looked around, her eyes wide, bewildered.

The woman in white leaned close to her ear. "This is Town Square Station," she said. "No money is exchanged in those stores and restaurants. But the people can get out and entertain themselves. Take things back for their homes."

Counselor Abagail watched the activity and slowly shook her head back and forth. A little girl chased a dog through brilliant green grass, through trees and scattered wrought iron benches.

"They worked very hard to keep everything the same as what your kind has been accustomed to."

As they stepped away from the tram station, Counselor Abagail looked upwards. The park in the center seemed to stretch farther than she could see. The sides were lined with busy shops and restaurants. There was a blue sky. Wispy, cotton-like clouds.

And she felt a breeze.

She leaned close to the woman in white. "This…is…*amazing*! You can't even tell that you're on a ship!"

The woman in white smiled and nodded as they found a bench on the edge of the square. She gestured, and Counselor Abagail sat. The woman in white sat next to her and smiled, making eye contact.

Counselor Abagail looked down, studying her hands, clasped in her lap, and then looked back up at the woman in white.

She was still smiling softly in silence.

Counselor Abagail looked the woman up and down. The woman was dressed like the others in her neatly pressed white uniform. She thought the woman might have been a nurse. But now, she felt this woman might be more of a guide. She finally asked the question that she had been wondering all along. "Who are you?"

The woman in white smiled and nodded. "I was wondering when you were going to ask me about my origins. My name is Inikia."

"You are a nurse? You helped me with that drainage bag…"

She shook her head.

"I am much more than a nurse," Inikia said, and pointed her chin out towards the many people. "Look around you," she said. "All those people out there. Everyone here is just as scared and confused as you are, but all have different assignments. A different purpose for being here. You, soon, will learn yours."

"And so you are assigned to me?"

She nodded. "I have been assigned to you for many years. Our kind has studied your kind and prepared for this mission. I know many things about your people. I am here to protect you. And to guide you on your journey."

There was something comforting about hearing those words. Everything still seemed so strange, so oddly surreal, but she thought it was helpful to have someone who was determined to keep her under their wing.

Counselor Abagail leaned forward, her elbows on her knees, and rested her chin on her palm. The little girl was still playing with the dog across the way. "I just still can't believe all of this."

Inikia leaned forward and met eyes with Counselor Abagail.

Counselor Abagail leaned back and shrugged. "Everything's been such a whirlwind. And nothing makes sense. A town square on a ship? Deep in space?"

Inikia smiled and nodded. "Yes. We have made strenuous efforts to ensure your comfort for the journey." Counselor Abagail looked out at the scene before them as Inikia continued explaining how the ship was the largest ship that mankind had ever seen or experienced, and that it was a rescue ship, though the mission had changed.

Counselor Abagail watched children walking puppies. Some teenagers walked in a group, throwing their heads back in laughter, walking down a sidewalk lined by brilliant green grass, retreating into a bookstore, next to a small café, where tables were filled with patrons enjoying coffee, pastries, and reading books.

She snapped her head back to look at Inikia. "Why don't they seem to have the same problem that I do?"

"Oh, you mean the amnesia?"

Counselor Abagail nodded.

Inikia smiled again softly. "They are merely passengers. They do not have the mission that you have been chosen for. You are quite important, and therefore, we must keep you ageless in this environment."

Counselor Abagail's face shifted and she cocked her head to the side.

Inikia continued. "Our destination will take several lifetimes to reach. The passengers must be as comfortable as possible while they are aboard our ship. Their environment must be as familiar as it was on Earth. They need to be able to reproduce, and live just as they were when they were living on Earth. Everyone that you see here, walking through the town square, will not live to see our ultimate destination."

"But I will?"

She nodded. "Yes. You will. You will because we have been holding you in cryogenic stasis, which has been rendering you ageless. You are the same as you were, physically, when you first boarded the ship back on Earth."

"How long have we been traveling so far?"

"Several years Earth time."

"And you said that you had to keep me ageless?"

She nodded again. "Yes, for your mission. You have been chosen for your mission which expands a vast amount of time. Your involvement in Sector B, which we researched to be the leading society on the planet, has made you a select. Along with the others who accompanied you from that Sector – Jeremiah Walter, Eli DeJesus, and Winston Joseph."

Counselor Abagail raised her hand and turned to face Inikia. "Wait a minute," she said. "You mean I know Eli? From before? And that guy Winston. Him too? He stood up in the briefing and said he remembered *everything*. Not once did he look back at me. How could I know him? And who is this Jeremiah Walter?"

"He is the young man with the close cropped blonde hair that stood in the lower row."

Counselor Abagail nodded. She leaned back, sighed, and looked back over at her. "So you're saying I know him as well."

She nodded.

Counselor Abagail scoffed, looking down, staring forward. She shook her head. "And I just met you. At least officially." She looked up and made eye contact with the mysterious woman.

She smiled and looked downwards. "You have been a very nice case."

Counselor Abagail raised her eyebrows. "Oh," she said. "Thank you...I think." She looked Inikia in her eyes. "Since we are complimenting each other, I have to say, your name is quite beautiful.

Inikia smiled, and looked downwards. "Yes," she said. "Thank you. It is. But I must finish what I was assigned to do. I was to bring you to breakfast. You will see the others there that we spoke of. Now you know that you have a history with them. A long and deep history."

Counselor Abagail and Inikia headed down the Town Square to the Breakfast Hall – which was nestled between a deserted Pub and a bookstore. It was single door which opened to a long, dark hallway. There was a light which emanated from the far end. "Just head forward and I will get the others," Inikia said as Counselor Abagail ran her hand against the wall. It appeared to be made out of stone.

"Stone walls on a space ship?" She looked at Inikia, and could see the whites of her eyes in the dim light.

"There are many things about this ship that will seem quite foreign to you and your people," she said. "But we keep things very natural, at least in this central location on the ship. We spend our lives on these vessels, traveling through galaxies. We try to keep some of the common gathering areas as natural feeling as possible."

They reached the Breakfast Hall.

The small, dark hallway opened up to a large, brightly lit dining area which was lined with long, rectangular tables. At the far end of the cafeteria were expansive windows, along the hull. A black sea of stars was visible through the windows. There was a sea of 'Those Dressed in White', sitting at the expansive, rectangular tables. Counselor Abagail gasped when she looked past the dining members. "You!" she pointed. "I know you! I mean before this morning. Before your lecture. I *know* you!"

The man who approached her was also dressed entirely in white. She recognized him. It was Moses from the amphitheater. Up close, she could see the details of his appearance. His hair was shoulder length, dark brown and mussed, his facial hair noticeable but well-trimmed. "Yes, I would imagine you would," he said. He smiled and stepped closer to her. "Do you remember me from Sector B?"

She took a break and tried to remember. She studied his look, his smile, his hair, his build. She couldn't quite place him. But she knew that he had been familiar.

"I certainly remember you from the briefing," she said. "I heard what you said. I listened to your lecture."

He nodded and smiled. "Ah, yes. But I go deeper into your past, Counselor Abagail."

"My past, it seems, right now, is a mystery."

Moses grabbed a tray in the line and looked back at her. "But certainly, you must remember…something? Am I correct? You have this sense of familiarity with me, right?"

She nodded.

She tried to place him.

There was something about him that was familiar. Reassuring. She felt that the due to the fact that he was there, in this foreign and unsure environment.

That everything was going to be okay.

"Hey…Abby…I have a question for you."

She looked up from studying the food offerings. It looked oddly familiar. There were bright, yellow scrambled eggs.

Toast.

There even looked to be some breakfast potatoes.

"You have all this? In space?"

He smiled. "We are not all that different from you." He grabbed a pair of shiny tongs and placed a piece of toast on his plate. He offered another piece to her and she nodded. "So I have a question for you," he said. After a pause, the voices and the activity of the cafeteria seemed to fade away.

"Do you have what it takes?" he asked. "To be a leader?"

Her face shifted as they found a table. "I…"

He placed his tray on the table, sat down, as she did, and then he looked up at her, chewing on some bacon. "I see the qualities in you, Abby.

113

You can lead this team. I know you can. I saw it back on Earth in Sector B. Whether you remember or not, and I think in time, you will, you were in a leadership role in your colony. We've studied you. Over years. This is not a rash decision. It wasn't a rash decision even to save your kind."

She looked up. "What do you mean…save our kind?"

In her mind, an image flashed: she saw a massive wave coming towards her. It was fleeting, and then it was gone.

She shuddered, opened her eyes, and looked back at him.

He was sitting across from her, smiling, holding a steaming cup of coffee, his eyebrows raised. "Are you starting to remember?"

She shook her head, looking down at her half-eaten plate. She placed her fork down. "I…"

"You could be having a memory," he said.

He leaned forward.

"And I want to ask you, dear Abby, are you remembering something…right now?"

She closed her eyes.

In her mind, she saw a wall of water rushing towards her. She shuddered and opened her eyes. "I remember the wave," she said as he nodded.

"That's progress, Abby." Moses raised his head and looked up.

"Inikia," he said. "Thank you for bringing them over."

Jeremiah, Winston and Eli each sat down with a breakfast tray full of food. Moses picked up a small, white pot and held it up in front of them.

"Coffee?"

The breakfast table was awkwardly silent until Moses started a conversation about the ship. That got Eli and Jeremiah both commenting about how they found the corridors interesting, how Town Square was fascinating, and how they each loved the views of space through the hull. Counselor Abagail listened and watched as Winston raised his eyes and looked at her. He spoke softly, underneath the rather benign breakfast table conversation; he drew her attention. "You'll remember soon."

There were no specific revelations at the table, other than they were the selectees for the Mars mission. Moses discussed the reason why each of them were chosen.

Each of them had undertaken significant roles in Sector B.

They got up as Moses started walking towards the bay of doors on the other side of the Breakfast Hall. Counselor Abagail made eye contact with Jeremiah as he swung around and followed Moses. "This actually sounds exciting!" he said. "I still can't believe we were chosen!"

She extended her arm and ushered Eli and Winston along as they made their way through the sea of white; of the dining faces who were similar, yet so vastly different than those in the Town Square.

"Inikia," Counselor Abagail said. Inikia walked close to her, shoulder to shoulder, and leaned her head close towards Abby's.

"Certainly there were others, weren't there, Inikia?"

She looked up at Abby. "Others?"

She went on to explain how she couldn't understand that Sector B had been the only society with scientists. As the doors on the opposite wall swung open, Moses stood waiting, facing them, his hands clasped behind his back. Jeremiah stood next to Moses, beaming a smile and nodding.

Moses chimed in. "You four are the most qualified. And the fittest as well. Your endurance will be tested, Counselor Abagail. You are now the youngest. That's why we have been keeping you in cryogenic stasis. Your qualifications back on Earth make you essential to our team."

Inikia nodded and made eye contact with each of them. "You have been chosen. You have a very important task."

"And we will be entering areas of the ship which are prohibited for the other humans on the ship. You are getting a key to the inside."

They exited the Breakfast Hall to a long, white corridor. There were others dressed in white, but this hidden network of corridors were not as wide as the public halls near the residences; nor were they as busy.

It was far quieter.

Counselor Abagail thought she could hear the steady hum of the ship. And faint audio tones every few minutes. "Is that some sort of an alarm?" she asked.

Moses turned around. "They are proximity tones. We are close to Mars orbit. And not far from the bridge."

Winston tapped Jeremiah on the shoulder. "I know why they wanted us. Remember I said I remember everything?"

Jeremiah nodded.

"You're the botanist," Winston said.

Counselor Abagail's eyes widened. "You're not leaving us there, are you?" Both Moses and Inikia laughed.

"No," Moses said. "Not in the least. We have been planning this mission for our kind since before we arrived in Earth's orbit. And we have continued to modify the pressure suits and procedures to benefit your kind the past two years you were in stasis. Your natural knowledge for Geology and Meteorology will be a great asset to this mission. Now please, all will be explained at the briefing."

They arrived at a single door which opened after Moses waved his open hand in front of it. The team crept forward, and Counselor Abagail was first to enter the room. A white bearded man dressed in white sat on the far end of a long, rectangular conference table.

A large screen in the center of the table displayed a graphic of the red planet that they were hovering close to. As they slowly entered the room, the man stood, smiling, and walked over towards Counselor Abagail, extending his hand.

"Copernicus," he said, smiling and nodding. He greeted each of them, giggling and giddy. Quite happy to see them. He looked over and made eye contact with Moses. "So this is our team?" There was a twinge of excitement in his voice. His long, white beard moved back and forth when he spoke.

Moses nodded as Inikia showed each of them to their seats. Counselor Abagail looked across the table at Jeremiah who leaned over to smell the leather as he sat in his chair, with an exaggerated inhale.

Counselor Abagail shook her head and took her seat.

It was soft, comforting and supple.

She could smell the fresh scent of the leather waft upwards as the cushion expanded beneath her. "Some things are not adding up for me. And possibly not for the other members of our team."

Copernicus raised his eyebrows, now sitting back at the head of the conference table, as the others took their seats. Moses sat down next to her.

"Like these leather chairs, for example?"

"What about them?" Copernicus asked.

"What is it made from? Cosmic cows?"

Copernicus smiled, nodding. "Is the idea so far-fetched?"

She looked over at Jeremiah as he shrugged his shoulders and shook his head. Eli was sitting next to Winston, both of them watching her.

Counselor Abagail continued. "What about your name? Copernicus? Like the astronomer?"

Moses leaned closer to Copernicus and smiled. "Exactly like the philosopher, am I right?" He patted the old man lightly on his shoulder. Copernicus was strumming his beard, leaning back in the chair. He looked straight at Counselor Abagail, apparently waiting for her to say something else.

He stopped strumming his beard. "Will you trust us, Abby? Will you take the leap of faith?"

Her mouth dropped open as she wheeled her chair close to Jeremiah. She leaned in close to him. "I remember something!"

Jeremiah's eyes widened.

She looked up directly at him as he sat back in his chair. "I remember when you were telling me about the star!" Her speech shortened, pitched higher and increased in volume. She looked back and forth from Copernicus to Moses and again focused on Jeremiah as she spoke. "Yes! You told me about a star! That you were having visions!"

Copernicus leaned forward, as Counselor Abagail lowered her arms and looked back over at him. He folded his arms. "Do you see?" he asked. "Your memory will return, in time. Little things like that may trigger it. Or they may not. But will you trust us Abby?"

She felt all eyes on her until Winston spoke and broke the trance.

"I remember everything," he said, clearing his throat. "And I do know that Jeremiah talked about a leap of faith. Back in Sector B."

Jeremiah's face lit up and his eyes widened. "We were going to head *North*!" Counselor Abagail raised her eyes and studied Jeremiah. So young and naïve, wasn't he? At least he appeared that way. Clearly excitable, but also fit. Was he former military? And what a revelation. She was supposed to have known him? How deep was their relationship? Was it professional?

Or could it have gone beyond that?

Copernicus stood and walked over to the side wall. "Enact visor!" he called out. The wall faded away, to an expansive display of Mars.

122

The red planet was a stone's throw away, surrounded by a field of tiny, white stars. Eli gasped and jumped from his chair as a massive asteroid filled the screen, flying across.

Copernicus let out a whistle and looked over at Moses and Inikia. "That came mighty close," he said.

Moses nodded. "The deflectors had to be disengaged. We're too close to Mars."

Copernicus nodded and headed back to the front of the room as Eli took his seat again. He stood in front of the table and clasped his hands behind his back.

"So let's get back to our mission," he said.

He looked out at each of them, sitting around the table. "Do you know why we are here?"

Silence followed, as Counselor Abagail looked at each of her team members. They were all focused intently on Copernicus.

"Anyone?"

Counselor Abagail cleared her throat as the others glanced over at her. "You said were we were scheduled on a mission to the surface. But why?"

Copernicus smiled and nodded. "Yes, yes."

He walked to the side, stared out at the red planet, his hands still clasped behind his back. After a few minutes, he turned back to face the group. He made eye contact with each of them as he spoke. Eli craned his neck up to see him.

"We have been studying your kind for many centuries," he said as the graphic in the center of the table zoomed in. "And we learned, over time, that mankind explored Mars quite extensively, until they launched a single, final mission. The SALVATION, I believe it was called. And during that mission, built a station in an area of the planet called *Utopia Planitia*."

"Utopia Planitia?" Eli asked. He leaned forward, looking down over the center of the table as the graphic zoomed closer in on a large surface area, covered with craters and sharp edged mountains.

"Yes," Copernicus said as the others looked for a few minutes, and then leaned back in their chairs. They looked up and refocused on him.

"Utopia Planitia is an area of Mars that is thought possibly to harbor life. There are indentations on the surface that indicate that water may have flowed on the surface at one point. Tiny ridges in the sand. Of sea beds and river beds that may have dried up billions of years ago."

"And where there's water," Winston said, "there can be life."

Copernicus nodded. "Exactly!"

Moses leaned forward, making eye contact with each of them. "And man wrote Mars off to be a dead planet. We have reason to believe that it is actually teeming with life."

He sat down and looked at the team in the eyes. Counselor Abagail studied the man intently as he spoke.

"Now man explored Mars for decades until their own planet started its demise. But the Earth you left behind is not the Earth that you were born into."

The graphic changed to the blue planet. "You all recall the orientation that Moses gave earlier?"

They nodded. "Yes, we remember," Counselor Abagail said. "The land on Earth formed a massive supercontinent that spanned the equator as the oceans moved towards the poles." The graphic followed as the continents were initially joined, drifted apart, and showed the blue water shifting towards the poles and creating a land mass which surrounded the equator. The graphic rotated to show the phenomenon was planetary wide.

"The trouble you experienced was caused by the rotation of Earth slowing and eventually stopping. The rotation of your planet kept the surface water evenly distributed throughout the surface. When the rotation slowed, there was a gradual shifting. There was a migration – of sorts – of the water flooding the poles. And at the same time, the surface around the center became dry and barren. That's why you're here with us."

Eli's eyes widened. He stared forward and nodded. "I remember the wave," he said, looking around the table, a crack in his voice. "I remember when the wave came."

Winston placed his arm around Eli's shoulder. Eli's voice quivered as he looked over at Winston. "I remember you pounding on the door and shaking me awake. And standing next to you, looking over the railing and all my paintings were floating in the water downstairs…" He hung his head down as Winston reached over to wipe the tears from his cheeks.

"Your memories will return to you," Copernicus said. "As we stated. The memory loss is an unfortunate side effect of the current cryogenic cooling process. We are getting close to a solution, however. Our scientists are working on a preventative solution for when you go into cryogenic stasis again."

Counselor Abagail raised her eyes to Copernicus. "We are going under again?"

"Let's get back to the current mission," he said. The graphic on the table returned to the red planet. It swiftly zoomed back towards Utopia Planitia. "As man explored Mars, over the course of nearly a century, a lot was 'stored' at the Red Outpost in anticipation of a possible need to colonize beyond the Milky Way."

Counselor Abagail raised her eyes and looked over at Copernicus. She looked at the others around the room. Jeremiah was nodding. "I remember when it was on the news," he said. "When the SALVATION went up. It took them what…almost two years to get there?"

Counselor Abagail nodded. "Yes, I remember too." She was staring at the graphic in the center of the table. "Nothing was said of that, though. It was an exploration mission, at least I thought it was."

Moses stood and walked around the table, making eye contact with each of them. "But what you were not told…what your governments held secret, was that one of the directives of the SALVATION mission was to deliver the seeds for a new civilization on a new planet."

"And *your* mission is to retrieve it," Copernicus said. The graphic in the center of the table changed to a sleek, black space rocket. "Your mode of transport," he said. The graphic rotated and zoomed as each of the team leaned forward. Copernicus touched the side panel of the ship and it expanded, opening to reveal several cylindrical pods inside. "SB1. It's our technology which has been modified to allow for human interaction."

There was a vehicle which looked familiar. Large, round wheels, which reached up towards the shiny, metallic windows. Three wheels on each side. The graphic changed as the ROVER was depicted moving forward along a rocky, red Martian terrain. Copernicus stood and looked at each of them. "You have experience operating this type of ROVER. It's quite similar to the fleet you had in Sector B back on Earth, and if you don't remember, I assure you, memories will return to you, the longer you have been out of cryogenic stasis. You will remember."

"Something's not adding up here," Winston said.

Eli cocked his head to the side.

"What's not adding up?" Jeremiah asked.

Winston stood, maintaining eye contact with Copernicus the entire time. "We have an assumedly alien race telling us to carry out their mission of going to the surface of another planet using their technology which we know nothing about." He looked over at Jeremiah and Counselor Abagail. "Jeremiah, you may have the experience in Botany and Meteorology, and Abby, you may have the experience in Mind Exploration, but none of us have any experience in Astronomy."

"I studied it in college," Counselor Abagail said.

"But none of us are Astronauts," Eli added. Both Jeremiah and Counselor Abagail nodded, as Copernicus returned to his chair.

"And none of us have experience beyond theory," Winston said.

"Your concerns are understandable," Copernicus said, looking directly at Winston. Counselor Abagail watched their interaction as Winston looked over at Eli and then over at Counselor Abagail. Copernicus folded his hands under his chin, and also looked over at Counselor Abagail.

"We talked earlier about taking a leap of faith," he said. She looked at Copernicus, over at Winston and then back at Copernicus again.

Copernicus made eye contact with them both, looking first at Counselor Abagail, and then over at Winston. Jeremiah looked over at Counselor Abagail and shook his head.

"Look at the door over there, behind you," Copernicus said. Counselor Abagail and Jeremiah turned around in their seats.

"You each have the will to leave. To walk out of this conference room and you can join the others at the Town Square. But is that the choice you will make? Will you choose not to be a part of saving humanity?"

After the briefing concluded, Inikia left with Counselor Abagail, Winston, Eli and Jeremiah. Copernicus and Moses sat across from each other at the conference table in silence. There was a slight hum from the acceleration system. Moses turned off the screen as the hull shifted from the clear visual of the cosmos back to the white, stark wall.

"Do you think they're ready?"

Copernicus stood.

He took a deep breath through his nose as he walked towards the door. After a moment, he spoke. "It's like you've told them before. They each have to be ready to take a leap of faith. I have confidence in each of their abilities. But they need to find the confidence inside themselves. It's a tough decision, I'm certain of that. And I don't know what could happen on the surface. It's hostile territory. Everything from the Bridge is saying that the sandstorms are worse than they've ever been."

Moses nodded as the men exited to the corridor. The door slid shut behind them. As they walked together towards the Mars 1 preparation area, Copernicus patted Moses on the back. "How long have we been doing this?"

Moses whistled. "Wow, commander. You're asking me a question like that? How can I answer?"

Copernicus let out a chuckle. "You don't have amnesia do you?" They stopped walking and faced each other.

Moses laughed. "No, nothing like that." They resumed walking. "It's just been quite a long time."

"Exactly, my son. And their galaxy is nearing its end. It's just a period in time that they happened to be witness to. So many millennia, and here we are. Just as we are supposed to be. But now, they are the leaders of the survivors of their planet. Whether they know it yet or not, they are the greatest minds."

Moses nodded. "True, true."

"And we're here to usher them to the next world," he said. "But it is *they* who have to make the commitment. Not only to save themselves, but to save the human race."

"Do you think they'll find it? Down on Mars, I mean?"

Copernicus stopped walking and faced Moses. They looked into one another's eyes. "Do not worry, Moses. It doesn't matter if they find it or not. Because they won't know what it is, and even if they discover it, they won't hold the key."

5

MEETING OF THE MINDS

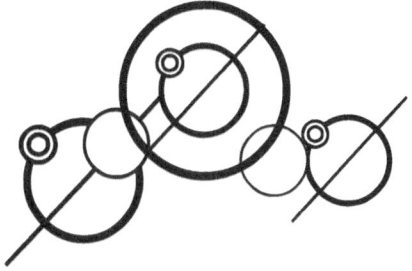

INIKIA STOOD IN THE CORRIDOR with her hands clasped behind her back. She stood across from the conference rooms, watching the team emerge from the sliding doors. She had led the procession from the briefing and turned and waited as the others exited slowly.

Her face was solemn; expressionless.

The wall glowed a pale blue behind her, and after they had left the conference room, a panel raised behind her to reveal a network of colorful alien foliage; blue, orange. Jeremiah ran to the edge of the wall, and pressed his face against the clear panel. "These are like nothing I have ever seen before!" He looked over at Inikia with wide eyes. "They are from the Lyra constellation. Perfectly natural for the habitat. The solarium gives them the proper lighting and nourishment."

"How did you know that?" Counselor Abagail asked.

"Memory triggers," Winston reminded. "Just like they said…you will see and hear things that trigger memories."

"We are hopeful that the amnesia will wear off soon and is only temporary," Inikia added.

Jeremiah's face was plastered across the glass covering the solarium.

He didn't appear to be listening.

He shook his head slowly. "But the temperature in that solarium?"

"It's similar to the mean average on your former planet, but a bit warmer. Also, our planet – or at least the planet that you will eventually colonize – has no magnetic shield. It's also slightly closer to its parent star –"

"– But what about radiation?" Eli leaned forward and looked over at Inikia with wide eyes.

Inikia moved closer to Eli. She placed her hand on his shoulder and leaned close to his ear. "You must learn to trust," she said. Counselor Abagail examined the plant life and watched Inikia attempt to comfort Eli. "It's a legitimate concern," Counselor Abagail said, as she studied a pink plant with large, round "leaves".

Inikia moved closer to the glass and stood next to Jeremiah, side by side, looking inside at the bright blue, pink, and orange colored shrubs and trees. "The species of foliage and forestry on the surface of this planet absorb stellar radiation. They dispel it as oxygen. That's one of the reasons why this will make it the perfect planet for you."

Counselor Abagail moved forward and joined them. She looked back at Winston and over at the others and they each agreed: the species of plants and trees were like nothing they had ever seen before. It was a patchwork of brilliant color; blues and purples, orange trunks, and no green foliage whatsoever.

Inikia reached her arm out and ushered the others to follow her. Jeremiah remained standing in front of the clear display, his mouth hanging open, his head shaking back and forth. Counselor Abagail leaned close to his ear and smiled. "You're a botanist," she reminded him. "At least that's what we've been learning. So I know you must be thrilled to see species that have never been seen by any humans before us."

He nodded slowly. "Yes," he said. "Just seeing that flooded my mind with memories."

"Please, let's go," Inikia said. "We must begin our sessions. It is critical that we understand you each in every detail before you begin your missions."

They followed her as Jeremiah reluctantly joined them. He looked back at the solarium repeatedly until it was out of view.

"So what's the deal with these mind exploration sessions you speak of?" Winston asked.

"You will each be interviewed as a group. And then be placed under sedation for an examination of your subconscious thoughts. And this process will help you recover your memories."

The team followed Inikia as she led them back to the Borderline tram, but as they walked, Counselor Abagail made eye contact with Jeremiah. He looked back at her and shook his head.

There, she knew it.

There was something strange about this mind exploration session. Could it help them? Or were there some other intentions that they were unaware of?

Their minds somehow connected.

They were led into a small room with chairs arranged in a circle. There was a small kitchenette off to the side with a coffee setup and cabinetry.

When they sat across from each other on the stark white chairs in the colorless room – save the expansive windows that opened towards the pastels and noble gasses of interstellar space.

But Abby ignored the celestial view.

She looked over at Jeremiah.

She saw him rub his close cropped blonde hair and watched him fidget. She thought that he could be former military, with the cut and the athletic build.

But with her memory only gradually returning with unpredictable triggers, she couldn't be for sure.

He looked downwards, towards the floor, draped his arms over the sides of the small plastic chair, and appeared to be speaking to himself. She looked down at his restless legs. The others were sitting in chairs opposite one another, patiently waiting.

"Hey," she said, leaning closer to Jeremiah. Her voice sounded somewhat foreign against the otherwise silent room. She noticed Winston and Eli looked up and over in their direction.

He stopped fidgeting and looked up at her with a blank expression on his face. "What is it, Counselor?"

She shifted in her chair, but maintained eye contact. "Back when we were standing outside the solarium, Inikia mentioned about mind exploration sessions. You looked over at me. Are you remembering something?"

He took a breath and sighed. "I'm not sure," he said. "I…"

She lowered her head but raised her eyes and maintained eye contact with him.

"I just don't understand any of this," he said. He shook his head and slouched back in his chair. "I don't get it. I wake up. We're in fucking *outer space*. No recollection of how we got here. And it seems that we are remembering things, but it feels they are older memories. From a distant past. What about more recent? Like how we got on this ship. Why is there a complete blank? But I don't know anything else. Except this." He gestured his arm out towards the room.

She nodded. "Except this."

He looked over at her. "I mean, is this what we have always been doing? Traveling through space on this ship?"

She shook her head. "No, it's clear we haven't. They speak of Sector B. But in every attempt to remember, I just get fleeting flashes, just tiny puzzle pieces, and I don't know how they fit together."

"But have you known anything different? Anything besides where you are and what you are doing right now?"

He lowered his head and closed his eyes. "This is all I am remembering. Waking up. A nurse of some sort came into my room. Connected some sort of drainage bag to the side of my knee. Going to see that Moses man. And then coming into this room."

The drainage bag.

So he had it too.

She folded her arms and cocked her head to the side, focused on Jeremiah. "So…why is it that we had to have a primitive bag draining *fluid*? I don't get it either. But you seem like you knew something back at the solarium."

"I don't *know* anything...I just go on feeling. And I don't know how I feel about these mind exploration sessions."

She nodded.

They both looked towards the door as Moses stood the doorway. He stood, smiling and nodding, his hands clasped at front of his waist. "So the entire team is here, he said. "Are you ready to get started?"

They each looked at each other but no one said anything.

Moses walked in the center of the circle of chairs. He looked at each of them as he spoke. "Since we have had amnesia issues since you woke, I think it's prudent that we do official introductions, so each of you are aware of who each of you *are*."

Winston raised his hand, stood, and Moses nodded at him.

"As I'd mentioned in the initial briefing, I remember everything," Winston said. "But if they are still experiencing amnesia, and only receiving memories in bits and pieces, how will they introduce themselves to one another?"

Moses smiled and nodded. "That's an excellent question." Winston sat back down, looked over at the others and shrugged.

"Eli DeJesus," Moses said, looking over at Eli. The young, Hispanic man looked up and cracked a smile. Moses then looked over at Abby and smiled. She looked up at him as he nodded. "Hi Abby."

The man with the close cropped hair stopped and leaned forward, looking up at Eli. "Wait a minute," he said. "You *know* her?"

"We met this morning," Eli said. "When we all went to listen to Moses. We sat next to each other."

Moses nodded. "I am well aware of that. But did you know that you have known each other for years? That you worked closely with each other back on Sector B?"

They looked at each other as Counselor Abagail made eye contact with Eli. "I thought you seemed familiar back at the briefing."

Eli nodded. "You too."

She looked over at Jeremiah. "And what about you?"

"I hadn't seen you in the amphitheater. But I feel that I know you."

"You each know each other," Moses said. "You each have a long history together, actually. Right Winston?"

Winston looked up at Moses and nodded. "Right," he said.

Counselor Abagail leaned back in her chair. The others took chairs across from her as she nodded to herself, as if deep in thought. "Yes...yes." Her face lit up as she made eye contact with the others. "I like that we're all on the same team. It seems...like it's was meant to be."

Copernicus headed down the corridor to the bridge. As he approached the outer atrium, a bay of doors slid open. There was a massive control center on the upper echelon, looking outwards to soaring windows which reached from floor to ceiling.

Mars was in view.

The crew were each at their stations. Copernicus stood in front of the large communication screen on the opposite wall. "Get me Moses."

CONTACTING MIND EXPLORATION LAB

It flashed a few moments across the screen as Moses appeared in the center. Behind him, Copernicus could see Inikia sitting in the group circle speaking with the team.

"It's time, Moses. We are ready. Get them ready. Now."

Moses nodded and the transmission ended.

No one knew if the Earth lived or perished.

As they explored each other's minds, their amnesia slowly lifted. They had discussed when the ship had just left Earth. How they could remember standing at the edge of what was to be known, on the ship, as 'Town Square'; at the far edge of the central area where there were vast observation windows.

They hung their heads as they left the expansive windows, as the arc pulled away and the blue sphere was no longer in view, gone. Inikia dimmed the lights. A hologram appeared in the center of the circle, showing the long, cylindrical ship. The ship exited the orbit, gaining speed, and moving away from the planet they once had known as home.

They all had agreed that there had been a star. It had been a wandering star; a collapsed celestial artifact that had somehow targeted their solar system – but as they had learned of the stars presence so late in the process, there was nothing that they could do.

"There was nothing you could have done, except leave," Moses said. "We detected the star far before you. And spent time researching your culture to prepare a new home for you."

A series of panels slid open on the opposite wall as the group looked over at Winston.

He leaned back in his chair with his hands clasped in his lap.

Inikia raised her eyebrows and studied him directly.

"So you have not experienced any type of amnesia from the cooling fluids?"

Winston shook his head and leaned forward. "I remember everything," he said.

"I remember when the scout – Moses – approached our colony. I can tell you that he was in poor physical condition and was immediately taken to Medical. The medical staff stabilized him as best they could and placed in him into quarantine."

Inikia ushered several others in white in the room. "What about what happened before Moses arrived?"

Inikia stood and approached the other side of the room. The panels retracted into the adjoining walls and revealed a room with four flat worktables surrounded by brightly lit monitors. She motioned to the staff and they scurried with several of the equipment panels as each worktable lowered slightly.

"Go on," she said, as the team's attention diverted back to Winston.

He cleared his throat. "I remember evacuating. When the wave came. We were close to the Eastern seaboard. Before the shift, we were probably 100 miles from the ocean. But when the wave came, we were coastal."

Jeremiah's eyes brightened. "Yes! I remember the wave too."

Inika stood next to the group of chairs and smiled. "You see, you can help each other. Each of you has been affected by the cryogenic process differently. But each of you can help the others remember. That will be critical, especially when you reach the surface."

Counselor Abagail was the first to undress.

The medical staff assisted her on the worktable, and she was covered in a shiny, metallic material. Several assistants inserted needles into her arms as the monitors behind her came to life.

"Open your mind to us, Counselor Abagail…let us see you…your history…your future…"

She closed her eyes and thought she saw a star.

A wandering star.

One of the neutrons that traveled through the galaxy, a white, hot sphere, with spirals of light fingering outwards. She hovered in its path, floating; levitating; coasting through the cosmos, as the planets whished past her: she felt the heat from the star, and turned around to the brilliance of the sun; towards the center of the Milky Way and beyond…

In some way, but they didn't exactly know how…they were all looking at the same thing.

Seeing the same visions.

Thinking similar thoughts. They had the same eyes. And ears. The ears were in the same spot on their heads; just beneath the hairline. For they were both men and women.

Humans, at least on the outside.

But what of the Vegans?

So similar…yet different. What had been their cosmic origin?

And many of them still looked the same.

Could pass as human.

Like the others, who really were humans, from the dying planet they had just visited, to save, to rescue, to bring to their ship.

But there were the others.

There were those who were already on the ship.

The Vegans, who had seen the humans from Earth file into the ship. They saw the same humans who had visited the quarantine lines, who were checked by doctors, and still, the Vegans who observed, who were already populating the ship, watched as the new humans filed inside, and once were medically cleared, were ushered into the living quarters. But that area, the living quarters, was where the new arrivals appeared to be most impressed.

They looked upwards at a soaring blue sky, one that mimicked what they had seen on their own home planet. The brilliant green grass never needed to be mowed, never needed to be watered.

There was one particular inhabitant of the ship, who stood in the grass, watching the new arrivals populate the ship and find and struggle to listen to – as some pressed their noses against the glass to say their final goodbyes to the blue planet.

Another vision came.

She saw herself, on the ship. Had it been more recent?

There was her mornings in the darkness. And the confusion. Her wake up time.

The day would continue; each day the same way. They would wake, drain the fluid from their knees, be escorted by a private nurse to their closest dining hall, eat breakfast and come alive once again.

But the same dreams and the same visions would not be remembered, nor discovered, until the group sessions later in the day.

And then, as the day wore on, they would start to remember. The haze would gradually lift. They would remember their days on the Earth.

It would slowly return.

In bits and pieces, broken memories and partial scenes, until, by the time the sessions ended and they adjourned for dinner, they were talking amongst each other; those who had been strangers upon waking remembered one another once again by the time they retired.

And when they would fall asleep, there would be darkness. No dreams that they could remember. And when they awoke the next day, the process would start all over again. They would have the same conversations with their private nurses. Completely devoid of any memory of the previous day; or how they got on a ship in the deep, dark vastness of space. Or even that they have ever lived on planet Earth ever.

And the same process would repeat itself in a cycle. Day, after day, after day.

How would this time be any different?

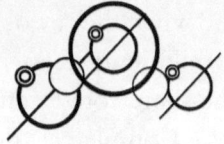

SHE WANTED TO OPEN HER EYES but she thought not to.

There was something different though. About the feel of the wrap.

Like it had been removed.

And she felt wind against her face. Had she been dreaming again?

She opened her eyes.

Before her were countless tiny, white stars.

But she was floating.

She looked around, gathered her senses, and gasped as she looked down at her legs: for the sea of tiny, white stars was endless; there was no beginning, nor was there a terminus. It was the vast beauty of space.

She turned around.

No ship.

Yet she was floating, gently, like rolling on waves, through space. …But where?

In the distance of space, she saw it. A tiny pin point of light. But this one was different from all of the others; it was brighter, seemed hotter. Out-bursting, bright, white-hot gases surrounded it, reaching outwards as it traveled closer to her.

You are the chosen one.

She watched the star. As it came closer. And a flood of memories permeated her mind. She remembered the North beach on the new continent back on Earth; she remembered Jeremiah sitting with her at their camp, the howling winds flapping at their tent. She remembered standing on the beach with him as their campfire embers were almost completely burned out. She remembered pointing up towards the sky, watching the bright star, as it dominated the sky, coming closer…and closer.

You are special. You are unique.

Beams of light flashed around her and past her as the star neared. She felt like there was no longer any force keeping her stationary; like she was falling into darkness that was surrounded by light. There were rings around the star; it swirled white-hot, and inviting.

As she fell, she outstretched her arms. Closer and closer she fell, through space, caught and there was no reason to leave. The warmth surrounded her, its fingers reaching across her, caressing her body, the wind blowing along her face.

Oh, my star. Oh, my love. Oh, my dream. May I never awaken again...

She opened her eyes and Moses was standing above her. He leaned in close to her ear and whispered to her. "Now you are ready, Abby. You are each ready for your mission."

She propped herself up on her elbows, looking over at the others. Eli and Jeremiah were just opening their eyes as well, as the medical staff had been removing the shiny metallic material from their bodies, and removing the needles from their arms.

"Psst! Jeremiah!" She watched as he covered his face with his hands. "My amnesia has lifted. I remember everything now!"

He rubbed his face and looked over at her. "Did you see what I saw?"

She closed her eyes and nodded. "It was so…beautiful!"

"I remember standing on the beach with you, Abby. You were the closest to me, remember? My confidant."

"And Cane!" she exclaimed as the medical staff assisted her into a white robe. "Desmond Cane! I can't believe I had forgotten about him!"

Inikia appeared next to them as Winston and Eli put on robes as well. The team stood before her, waiting and ready. "Your minds have been repopulated with the lost information," she said. "The cryogenic freezing process has been corrected. When you go back into hibernation, on our journey to Europa, we do not expect to have this effect any longer."

"For now," she said, "you must rest and eat. Later today you are scheduled for training on the mission pod for entry, descent and landing. Once you are on the surface, the ROVER will be the same that you are already accustomed to. But the Martian terrain is quite different. Much more hostile."

Later, back in the Dining Hall, Counselor Abagail stared at her vegetable soup. She picked up her spoon and stirred the red broth, examining the colorful vegetables. And then she felt the pressure on the bench next to her. Body weight.

She looked up slowly and saw the smiling blonde young man. He nodded at her and set his tray down next to hers.

"Oh, hello, Jeremiah."

He smiled and dug into his meal.

He took a few bites and leaned over closer to her. "How do you feel about this?"

She looked up and over at him.

"It's kind of bland. But palatable."

He chuckled and looked at her. "I mean all this." He waved his fork around as he spoke. "This whole mission that we're a part of." He took another bite, was chewing and looking back at her.

"I…" she placed her spoon down. "I'm not sure, Jeremiah. I mean, before the mind exploration, I hardly even knew who I was. It a pretty scary prospect. But now…"

"Now?"

"Now that our memories have been restored, and I know who I am, and where I came from, it *seems* like we are the perfect candidates to go."

Jeremiah took a long gulp of his water. "But why us? Why not them?"

She placed her spoon down for a moment, looking upwards, biting her bottom lip. "I think…" Then she looked back down into Jeremiah's eyes. "I think it has to do with us. And humankind. This is our task. It's our mission to complete. They could do it for us, I'm sure. Their technology appears to be much further along than ours ever was. But this is our mission. This is for our people. Our destiny. And I believe we need to be placed in the driver's seat for this one."

Jeremiah nodded as the hiss of hydraulics emanated from behind them. All heads turned around as they saw Moses, the rather modest looking man standing in the doorway. His hair was neatly parted on the side; his face was now clean-shaven. He was wearing the same standard issue attire that the other crew had been wearing: dark blue casual with heavy, black boots.

So was he was one of them?

Counselor Abagail watched Moses as the hydraulic doors hissed closed. He walked slowly towards the front of the Dining Hall, and paused for a moment, looking out at everyone, who had since stopped eating.

"Everyone," he said. "I want to introduce to you two members of our exploration team who are preparing for EDL currently. The other two members are now in training prep for the pod as engineers. But here, we have Counselor Janine Abagail, and Mr. Jeremiah Walter. Counselor Abagail will be leading the mission, and Mr. Walter will be focusing on DNA harvesting, seedling acquisition and transport."

He extended his arm out to where they were sitting and the entire hall erupted in thunderous applause as Moses sat down across from them.

As the applause died down, he leaned across the table, closer towards them. "We'll need you to report soon. But finish your lunches. Relax for a bit. It's going to be pretty intense from this point forward."

"I'll bet," Counselor Abagail said, taking a sip of water. "So why the grand introduction? Made me feel like I was some dignitary or something!"

Moses nodded. "To us, you are." He leaned a bit closer as Jeremiah leaned in as well. "You see, you are not the only ones we have rescued. But you are some of the first to see how necessary it is for one's own kind to take a significant role in ensuring their future, and discovering their destiny."

"Wow," Jeremiah said. "There are others?"

Moses nodded and leaned back. "Yes. There are others. We have been doing this for…I cannot even fathom, it seems."

Counselor Abagail's mouth dropped open as she pushed her bowl forward. "Are you Vegan? Or Human?"

"Good question, Abby," he said. "And I will give you the best answer that I can. I am Moses. Copernicus is Copernicus. We are who we are.

This is who we were created to be. I cannot say that we are truly Vegan – because our entire existence is on this ship."

"But what about the others?" Jeremiah asked. "The crew, Inikia?"

"Inikia is a Vegan. She volunteered for this ship's mission so long ago, it seems. There's less of a concept of time here, you know? Since we're always out exploring the cosmos. Making the occasional stop, and drop off. Bringing cultures who are on dying planets to new ones to start over…but never really use the measurement of time."

They nodded.

"I can see that," Jeremiah said. "Time passes so differently based on where you are in the Universe."

"Exactly," Moses said. He stood. "Now take a few more minutes. Relax. Inikia will be coming shortly to pick you up. Copernicus has been calling for the final preparations for your mission."

After they finished their lunch, Inikia came to escort them to BAY 1. They were led down the longest, windowless corridor that Counselor Abagail could remember. Unlike the rest of the ship, this corridor was dark and grey. Networks of panels were on the walls every ten to twenty feet, and at each panel, a team of those dressed in white were manning the stations. The corridor opened into an expansive hanger. Her mouth dropped open as she looked out to see a massive set of doors, clamped shut. In the center of the receiving bay, she saw Eli and Winston already suited up in heavy, white space suits. Their helmets sat on a small table next to them.

"Last chance to use the bathroom!" Eli called out and started waving when he spotted them. Copernicus and Moses stood with them.

"That goes out towards the unknown," Copernicus called out, pointing at the large horizontal doors. And then he looked at the rest of the team. "Just wanted to let you all know how close you are."

Jeremiah looked up and saw the underbelly of MACA 1. "Holy shit!" he exclaimed. And then he looked over at Winston and Eli. You guys are going to pilot *that*?"

MACA 1 was massive in its own right. It looked just like the hologram back in the conference room. Sleek, black, pointed nose.

"It actually will pilot itself," Winston said. "There's practically no room for error."

Counselor Abagail approached the others. "But something could go wrong, couldn't it, Copernicus?"

"This scenario is routine," Copernicus explained. "Winston and Eli have been trained on scenarios where they may need to initiate a manual landing. But the chances of that are extraordinarily rare."

"Let's not think about that," Jeremiah said.

As Jeremiah and Counselor Abagail approached the others, Inikia instructed them to go to the left dressing chamber to use the facilities and dress. "In your suit, you will be connected to catheters for bladder relief while on the surface. There are facilities at The Red Outpost, but there will be no opportunity to remove your suits and helmets on this particular mission."

"Well, shit, I can't take a piss," Jeremiah said. "Now what am I supposed to do?"

"Countdown in T-minus 10 minutes."

Counselor Abagail looked down at the control panel, which reached around where she stood in a semi-circle. She looked down at the flat, black screens which covered the top of the command station, as she touched the screen furthest to the left.

INITIATE SEPARATION.

She held her hand just above the screen for a moment, just a few inches above the glass, as the words flashed their urgency in red.

As she stood and waited for the separation command, Jeremiah, Eli and Winston were in the outer chamber. Jeremiah closed his eyes as an aide snapped the pressure suits together. Jeremiah could feel a cooling breeze, a light circulation of air.

"Check your oxygen levels." The aide's voice was muffled, but recognizable. Jeremiah opened his eyes. Now that his helmet was on, the darkness surrounded him. He could see the controls through the viewing window; a sea of colorful, blinking lights.

The massive hydraulic doors lifted open.

He had never been in the vastness of space before. At least not that he could remember. He turned and watched the aide check his notes through the visor.

"EDL seven minutes," Counselor Abagail said, monitoring the controls as MACA 1 separated from the ship. She turned around in her seat and faced Winston and Eli as Jeremiah focused on flying the spacecraft.

She looked at them both strapped in their seats and saw Eli was panicking. She could see through the visor that his eyes were wide. She looked down at his hands and they were grasping the seat.

"Calm down, Eli. We'll be fine."

He closed his eyes and shook his head back and forth. "What's EDL?" He repeated it over and over as the ship roared to life, taking them closer to Mars.

She reached out and touched his knee as he opened his eyes and looked up towards her. "It's Entry Descent Landing," she said. "Now listen, Eli. We will be fine. Jeremiah has been trained again and again on this spacecraft and on entering Mars atmosphere. But I need you to be calm. We'll be on Martian soil in seven minutes."

She turned around in her seat, secured herself, and looked over to Jeremiah. She waved her hand and they switched to a secure channel. "Are you ready for this?"

He looked over at her, cracked a smile, nodded. She noticed how his giant white helmet bobbed up and down. But she saw the smile. And he gave a thumbs up.

Jeremiah spoke as he commanded the spacecraft.

"Ready. Descent. Initiate."

She looked out at the red planet below them in the viewfinder. It looked like a giant, red sphere hovering in a black space. But in seven short minutes, they would be landing.

And not much after that, they would be walking on the sandy soil.

4

WE ARE ALL JOVIAN

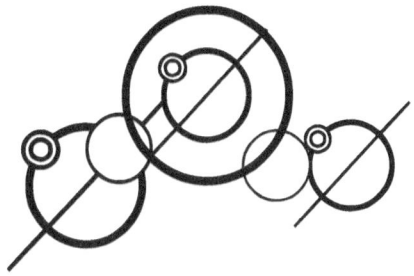

COUNSELOR ABAGAIL TURNED AWAY from the dark mountain, facing the horizon. The sandstorm had abated, but the light was fading. The surface would soon be enveloped in darkness. She typed on her forearm keypad, and shortly after, a series of commands appeared on the dark edge of her visor, along with a digitized voice:

ROVER LOCATION COMMENCING.

She paused and waited for a moment as a small icon rotated in the center of the screen. The text flashed in and out.

"Jeremiah? Winston?"

Her voice sounded small, and tinny. They probably couldn't hear her through the tiny microphone transmitter. Or could they?

Or were they buried in the three graves behind her?

She paused for a moment.

Had she had another memory lapse?

There was a period that she spent on the surface of Mars before the team had lost each other. Shortly after they had landed at Utopia Planitia, with a mission destination of the Red Outpost, she had spotted the ROVER. It stood on the red sand, a silver beacon, reflecting the light from the muted sun. The ROVER appeared as if it were the only sense of familiarity in this foreign, hostile land.

As she walked against the cloud of blowing sands, several maps lighted on the dark interior of her helmet, to the side of the visor:

ATMOSPHERE PREPARATION IN
PROGRESS!

It flashed as the digitized female voice spoke the update in her earpiece, in a methodic tone, spaced out by several second intervals.

The ROVER was only a short distance away. It reflected the muted sunlight through the blowing sands, almost glowing against the dim atmosphere.

She reached her arms outwards towards the vehicle.

ATMOSPHERE PREPARATION IN
PROGRESS!

Struggling against the force of the wind, she crossed her arms across her chest, the hard upper torso of her spacewalk apparatus. She moved forward, as each determined step took her closer to the ROVER.

The ROVER appeared so close; but through her visor, she could see it was parked beyond the far ridge. It shined at the base of a soaring plateau; it gleamed against the fading light; its silver hue seemed to glow, if not shine.

Her footsteps were determined and certain. There was no other destination that she could think of.

The ROVER was there.

It did not matter how she had gotten on the surface of the Red Planet. For the ROVER, the shining beacon in the dim, fading light of Mars, was the only sense of familiarity in a foreign world.

She paused once she reached the proximity of the ROVER. A few yards shy, she saw it sitting there.

Lightless, motionless.

Appearing as if dead.

As the winds picked up once again, blowing the sand against her visor.

She raised her hands and wiped it clean.

"Clear code for communication," she said. Her voice reverberated against the helmet interior sphere and her voice sounded tinny in the COM lines. "Jeremiah?"

No answer, just the howl of the winds.

She trudged forward to the ROVER, and fell against it, catching her breath. The front door was flush. She reached out and ran her hands against the edge.

No handle.

She took a breath and sighed.

But she knew she had to get inside the ROVER. The winds were increasing in intensity. She looked back towards the dark mountain. It seemed so much farther away than she had thought; there was a large, shallow crater in the middle of the two mountainous formations. Had she really ventured that far? Had the ROVER truly shined like a saving beacon of light? As if highlighted by the Heavens?

She fumbled with the arm pad, typing in key combinations. The feel was muted and soft; her suit was bulky and did not allow for precision in her typing, but after several attempts, a small screen appeared on the inside of her visor.

OPEN ROVER?

It read.

"Command yes."

The text disappeared as the screen minimized to the corner of her viewing area. The side of the ROVER slid open. She approached cautiously but with determination. There were four seats amidst darkened controls. As the winds increased in intensity, she collapsed into one of the chairs near the front console. The side panel eased itself closed as the roar of the wind was reduced to a light howl outside the sealed chamber as the message screen on her visor maximized.

INITATION SEQUENCE COMMENCING.

The controls on the front panel lit across the dash in bright succession. The panel in the center lightened from a deep black to a light grey. She leaned forward to see a message forming in the center of the screen.

ATMOSPHERE PREPARATION IN PROGRESS.

Air blew through the interior as the exterior windows covered with sand.

A green light appeared in the side of her visor as the message flashed across her visor screen:

ATMOSPHERE AT SAFE LEVELS.

The green light flashed as she waited.

DISENGAGE?

She selected yes as the collar decompressed. She removed the helmet and dropped it on the floor.

The ROVER was covered in Martian sand. There were the remnants of clipboards and a visor screen in pieces on the floor, its colorful wires scattered in various directions. As she looked around the inside, desperately trying to get a greater memory of what happened before she woke at the bottom of the surface, she noticed the flashing message on the console screen:

AWAITING VOICE COMMAND.

"This is Counselor Janine Abagail."

The ROVER screen lightened as a digitized voice responded.

"Awaiting your directive Counselor Janine Abagail."

She looked up and around the interior. No speakers. Had she been speaking with someone on the ship?

She leaned back in the chair and took a breath. Air! Even if it were manufactured, and she couldn't breathe it outside, she came to a new appreciation of the Earth's atmosphere. She leaned her head back, closed her eyes, and sighed. And then she leaned forward and opened her eyes. "I am missing the other members of my team."

The monitor swirled for a moment.

"The members of your team are no longer living."

She gasped.

The image of the three mounds of dirt flashed through her mind. "ROVER. Can you locate the other team members? Where can I retrieve their bodies?"

"They are not able to be located. Their communication apparatus is dysfunctional, and not communicating. Recommend contacting Vega One and returning to mothership."

Were they truly gone?

"Are they gone? Where are their bodies, ROVER?"

There was another series of tones. "Their communication apparatus does not function. Their presence cannot be detected."

"ROVER, how do I contact Vega One?"

There was a series of audible tones. "Attempting location of Red Outpost."

She shook her head. "I need to contact Vega One."

"Your assigned mission from Vega One was to locate the Red Outpost and retrieve a genetic inventory left by human predecessors."

"Can we contact Vega One?"

"Contact from this vehicle is not possible. Carrier signal has been lost. Recommend return to Red Outpost immediately for contact with Vega One."

She nodded and looked out the windows as the sandstorm was quieting. The Martian terrain – red sand peppered with darker rocks – was coming more clearly into view. "Take me to the Red Outpost."

She looked out the windows as the ROVER slowly turned its wheels. She could hear the crunching gravel below. As the vehicle started traveling away from the dark mountain formation, she turned around, looking at where she had been. There had been no indication of how she got here.

But now, she had an idea.

As she looked outwards, the image of the three mounds of dirt permeated her mind. And the empty suit. It was Jeremiah's.

What had happened back there?

At the end of the mountain formation was a small structure. It was built into the side of the mountain, but was clearly not part of the terrain. She saw a silver glow; a reflection of the fading light, as the ROVER slowly navigated the rocks that peppered the sandy landscape.

RED OUTPOST APPROACH!

An audible alarm sounded. The voice increased in urgency.

DUST DEVIL PORT SIDE!

DUST DEVIL PORT SIDE!

She looked out towards the left. It looked like a swirling tornado; something she might have seen back on Earth. It looked to be several miles away, through the gap between the dark, sandy mountains.

It was a swirling dust cloud; much larger than any tornado she had ever seen.

"ROVER, what is that dust devil?"

There were a series of tones as the ROVER pulled into the camp. "A Mars 'Dust Devil' is a violently swirling cloud of dust that moves across the terrain. During the days of the SALVATION mission, the phenomena was studied by man and it was determined that they are similar to tornadoes on Earth, but dust devils are not associated with weather."

"And are they a threat?"

"Winds speeds can reach over 100 miles per hour and they are considered a threat to all Martian construction put in place by man."

"ROVER, which direction is it headed?"

"Counselor Abagail, it is currently stationary."

The audible alarm sounded again as the urgent voice rang above her.

OUTER DOOR OPENING IN T-MINUS ONE MINUTE!

She picked her helmet up from the floor and eased it over her head. As the neck panel clicked into place the interior lights came to life, and the oxygen chambers hissed full of air. As the side door slowly rumbled open, she looked once more through the other side of the ROVER. The dust devil stood there. A swirling plume of dust. She felt like it was mocking her. Had she much more time?

It was oddly calm around the RED OUTPOST. It was nestled in a crook of the mountain range; surrounded by soaring plateaus in a small, shaded corner of rock. When man had built this remote research and planning station, the scientists involved took great planning and preparation. Could the massive rock formations offer protection from the dust devils that moved across the rolling sands ahead?

As she approached the entry door, she turned around and looked at the swirling sand through the break in the rock formations. It was much further away than it appeared. Could the massive rocks break it apart?

She turned back towards the door.

She wiped a layer of dust from the access panel as a screen came to life. A digitized male voice greeted her.

"Welcome Counselor Abagail."

The door slid open with a hiss.

She took a step inside and looked at the surroundings. A receiving chamber of some sort. Other suits similar to the one she was wearing hung on the side wall. Large, heavy looking boots lined a floor which looked to be made of steel. And further in was a larger door, which looked to open horizontally. The male voice filled the room.

OUTER DOOR CLOSING.
ATMOSPHERE STABALIZATION
COMMENCING!

She looked back as the door slid closed with a thud. A series of red lights on the far wall illuminated in a pattern – three at a time, two at a time, four at a time, two at a time.

And then they all changed to bright green.

ATMOSPHERE AT SAFE LEVELS.

She unlocked the neck from her helmet as the pressurization hissed outwards in tiny plumes. As she lifted her helmet high above her head, she took a deep breath.

The air was perfectly breathable. Just as it had been in the ROVER. She treasured the air going in and out of her lungs. This place seemed somewhat familiar in this foreign world. And while there still was a great deal of mystery surrounding how she got to be here, she was hopeful that her memories would return. That things would start to appear familiar again.

Her thoughts were interrupted by the same voice:

INNER DOOR OPENING!

The door rumbled open with a hiss. She paused, looking across the threshold. The interior had several hanging lights that cast a warm glow on what appeared to be a long, rectangular work table in the center of a darkened room. Papers and electronic devices were scattered across the entire length of the table.

PRESSURIZATION COMPLETE.

She looked up towards the ceiling. There didn't appear to be any speakers – nor cameras – but she felt that she was being monitored. Observed. And then a familiar voice rang through the silence as she stepped into the darkened room.

CONTACT VEGA ONE?

It was the same voice from the ROVER.

She took a moment to clear her throat. "You…are you the same computer from the ROVER?"

I AM.

"And you followed me here?"

I AM ASSIGNED TO YOUR WATCHFUL PROTECTION.

"How is that possible?"

I WAS PLACED INTO YOUR HELMET ASSEMBLY, AND AM ABLE TO

CONNECT TO DEVICES WITH YOUR SIGNATURE.

She nodded and looked around the room. There was not much to see beyond the table. The hanging lights – which to her, seemed quite primitive in such a high tech installment – were weak in their light distribution. The light didn't reach beyond the center table, and the walls faded to darkness.

Papers were scattered about the table.

To her, it seemed out of place. They hadn't used paper for many years. How long had this outpost been in existence?

CONTACT VEGA ONE?

The voice filled the room.

"Uh…" she stammered and found a small stool. She dragged it out from under the edge of the table and sat down, bending her knees and resting her feet on the rung. "Computer, is there a communication station somewhere in this facility?"

THAT IS A NEGATIVE.

She raised her eyebrows and her mouth dropped open slightly, as she cocked her head to the side. "Oh…kay…so how am I supposed to contact Vega One?"

YOU ISSUE THE COMMAND AND YOU WILL BE SPEAKING WITH THEM.

She nodded slowly. "Speaking with them…I see…so I just say I want to contact them?"

YOU ISSUE THE COMMAND WHEN YOU ARE READY.

She shrugged her shoulders. "Okay. Contact Vega One."

The far wall lit up, like a giant screen in muted grey. There was a dull audible tone, and then she saw two men appear, in giant super lifelike appearance. One man had snow white hair and a matching beard; the other was clearly younger, with brown shoulder length hair. They both beamed. "Counselor Abagail! We thought we'd lost you!"

Her face shifted. "Come again?"

The snow white man spoke first. "Jeremiah thought you might have this issue. Do you have memory loss?"

She shook her head. "What do you mean? Jeremiah?" She thought of the empty suit back at the edge of the mountain. "I…woke up out of some slumber or loss of consciousness to a missing team. I honestly appear to be suffering from some sort of amnesia. I am starting to remember the others who were on the team with me, but I honestly don't remember you or how this mission began."

There was an interruption in the communication feed as the outpost shook and rumbled. She reached out and braced herself on the table and chairs. She raised her head towards the ceiling. "What was that?"

THE DUST DEVIL HAS APPROACHED
OUR LOCATION!

She ducked underneath the table as the outpost shook and rumbled once again. There was a howl of wind just outside. She raised her voice. "Computer! What is the scenario if the Red Outpost is destabilized?"

EXTERIOR WALLS WILL IMPLODE
DUE TO PRESSURE DIFFERENTIAL.
ANTICIPATED DEATH DUE TO LACK
OF ATMOSPHERE.

As the dust devil roared its ferocious winds, just outside of the Red Outpost, the walls shook and rumbled, as Counselor Abagail lay down underneath the table, drew her knees up to her chest, and shut her eyes tight. And in the midst of the roaring winds, as the walls felt as if they might buckle, a voice had entered her mind.

Fall forward. Trust. Take a leap of faith. And everything will fall into place.

She opened her eyes.

The underside of the table cast a shadow on her face. She took a breath. There still appeared to be an atmosphere. The walls must still be intact. She eased herself up on her elbows. "Computer?"

No answer.

She crawled out from underneath the table to see the same two faces on the far wall. Their eyes were wide. Once she emerged, the man with the white hair spoke. "Counselor Abagail! What is happening down there?!"

She hung her head down for a moment and shook her head. She sighed. "Dust devils," she said. "I had no idea what they were. But I asked the computer and was told they erupt in the Martian atmosphere with little or no warning. They're far larger than any weather phenomenon ever seen on Earth."

The younger of the two leaned forward, and his face filled the screen. "Nelson Moses here. I know you are having some memory issues. Do you remember me? We must get you out of there. We know about the Mars dust devils. I believe that's why that station had been abandoned."

She stood still, with her arms hanging at her sides. She raised her eyes and looked at both men. "I'm not going anywhere until you tell me where my team is."

She thought of the three graves back in the shadow of the dark mountains.

And the empty space suit. She couldn't find an explanation for that.

Copernicus beamed.

His eyes widened and he started smiling and laughing. "There is no reason for that, Abby! They are right here!" They have been with us for a while now. That's why I said I thought we lost you!"

She watched the far wall screen, the larger than life movie, of Copernicus, the old, grey haired man who seemed somewhat genuine, but she was having a difficult time remembering him. Nelson Moses, the younger of the two, significantly so, as his brown shoulder length hair dictated, she felt a closer connection with. There was something about him. She felt that she had known him. Sometime in the past.

Copernicus and Moses ushered the others into the view of the screen and her memory was instantly jolted. Her eyes widened, her face beamed and her mouth dropped open. "Jeremiah! Winston! Eli! What are you doing on the ship? The computer down here calls the ship 'Vega One'. But I honestly am having a hard time remembering anything other than the three of you."

Jeremiah moved to the front.

He was as she had remembered him. He didn't look injured at all. His skin was perfect. His blonde hair close cropped. "Counselor Abagail!" He beamed.

He flashed a big smile.

She shook her head. "I don't understand," she said. She looked directly into his eyes. The image of his face filled the back wall in a larger than life shot. "I woke up out on the sandy terrain. And I had no idea where I was, how I had gotten there. Nothing."

Jeremiah was nodding as she was speaking. "That makes sense to me," he said. "You had fallen down into a ravine. We thought we had lost you! You don't know how ecstatic we are to be communicating with you!"

She closed her eyes and shook her head. "Wait a minute, Jeremiah. You mean to say I almost died?"

"Yes. You almost died. We left Mars because we could not locate you. I don't know how deep you fell into the ravine, but we weren't able to rescue you. And after a great deal of time spent searching, we declared you dead."

Moses moved into the viewing area. "And we were so astoundingly pleased when we found out you survived! We are preparing a rescue mission at once!"

She looked up at the others on the screen. "Let me speak to Jeremiah. I need to speak to him in confidence."

Moses nodded. "Of course, of course! You need a private line."

She nodded.

"Okay then! Jeremiah go to 3.5.2.1. and we will have you set up for a private conversation within minutes."

She nodded. "Thank you."

"And for you? We need to return to the surface to rescue you."

She lowered her head and nodded. "I agree. Send the rescue ship. Get me off this planet. It's dead here. It's not like the Mars that I had heard about while growing up, when they said that there was life teeming under the surface."

"We will have the rescue pod down to the surface within minutes."

"And I will wait for my private chat with Jeremiah."

Moses nodded. "Absolutely!" he said. Copernicus appeared on the screen and was in agreement with Nelson. "You will get some time to speak with Jeremiah," Copernicus said. "When we are preparing this mission. And we will be down there soon. It won't take us long at all."

While waiting on Vega One, she ventured further into the compound. She left her helmet on the conference table. She walked away from the conference room, navigating the littered paperwork and the haphazard chairs. Across from the table, was a corridor, which led to a network of other corridors, further and further into the dark crevices of The Red Outpost.

The corridors were littered with debris and papers. This post had been abandoned for quite some time, she could tell. As she shuffled her feet down the metal corridor, she called out.

"Computer?"

YES COUNSELOR ABAGAIL.

"Can you direct me to the chamber where the DNA and seedlings are held?"

YOU MUST PROCEED FORWARD. AT PRECISELY TWENTY ONE YARDS AHEAD, THE DOOR TO THE DNA HOLDING CHAMBER WILL GRANT YOU ACCESS.

"Thank you computer."

She headed down the corridor and cracked a light stick. The greenish glow highlighted the narrow walls, the debris on the floor. It also cast a bit of green tinted light on the metal door on the far end of the corridor.

As she approached, it said:

NO ACCESS.

Who were they trying to keep out?

Standing in front of the door, she looked at the panel to the left. There was a small, silver plate.

"Computer? How do I access the DNA holding chamber?"

PRESS YOUR RIGHT THUMB TO THE PANEL.

The door slid open and she gasped.

It was like entering a tiny, tropical rainforest. There was foliage of all kinds, lining rows with a clear roof and artificial sunlight. How long had this been here? And the plants are still thriving?

She turned to the left.

There were chambers filled with test tubes and large freezer drawers. She took a few steps forward, and then there was a rumble.

She heard the exterior door open.

Had they arrived already?

She walked down the long, dark corridor and saw the light filtering through from the conference room. After seeing the chamber, she had many more questions. When were these items placed there? And for what purpose? Was man trying to seed another planet?

As the inner door slid open, she saw Jeremiah's smiling face. "They sent me to come get you," he said.

"We don't have much time, either. Out on the plain there are dust devils everywhere! One almost took out the pod!"

Her mouth dropped open.

It was Jeremiah all right. But he seemed…different.

She brushed the feeling of uncertainty off and rushed over and gave him a hug. He was still in his big puffy suit, and held his helmet.

Jeremiah wrapped his arms around her, and she placed her head on his shoulder. She felt the warmth of tears streaming down her cheeks. "I thought I was marooned here alone!"

He closed his eyes, rubbed her back and comforted her as she placed her head on his shoulder. "We thought we had lost you," he said. "We landed on the top of the plateau and you walked to the edge but lost your footing. When you fell, we had thought you died."

She shook her head. "I woke up with no memory of how I got here," she said. "My mind has been playing too many tricks on me lately."

He opened his eyes as she stepped back and sat in one of the small folding chairs. She shook her head slowly and then looked back up into his eyes. "There are so many things about this place that seem a little…off."

His face shifted as he took a chair and sat across from her. "What do you mean, Abby?"

She scoffed and cracked a smile. "Everything here," she said. "And what is one of the strangest things…is that I found *your* empty suit back by a mountain. My mind is drawing a blank."

"Are you sure you weren't hallucinating?"

She shrugged her shoulders. "I don't know. I suppose. I have been so lost since waking up here that I couldn't even remember what the mission was supposed to be."

"We were sent here to gather genetic DNA which was placed here at this facility."

She nodded. "Yes. I found it earlier. Do we still have to gather it before we leave?"

He stood and shook his head.

"No. We've already obtained plenty of samples. They're already back on Vega One. But we do have to get moving, Abby. We can talk more on the ship. The others are waiting for you as well. We were celebrating up there when we received your transmission. Copernicus was minutes away from leaving the region."

She sighed and followed him into the receiving chamber.

He helped her get into her space suit and pulled it up over her shoulders. As he handed her a new helmet, she paused and looked him directly in the eyes. "I just wish I could remember. Or find out what is real and what is not."

Jeremiah nodded and put his helmet on. She followed suit. After a few moments, the helmet interior lighting came to life. And then he spoke to her over the audio address system.

"Nothing here matters anymore," he said, as he turned around and pressed the panel. The door slid open to high winds and blowing red sand. He turned to face her. "We got what we came for. And we got you back. Mission complete."

She bit her lower lip as she followed him into the winds. She cursed her faulty memory, and still could not understand the amnesia. When she watched Jeremiah open the side door of the rescue pod, she still thought he seemed a little different. He looked like Jeremiah. He walked and talked like Jeremiah. He just seemed a little different. Had something happened to him?

As she strapped herself into the co-captain's chair, she looked back at the camp. The ROVER was still sitting in the same spot that she left it. Would it be destroyed by dust devils?

And as the pod lifted into the Martian sky, she watched the terrain get smaller. And then she thought she saw something. Near the dark mountains. There was a glow in the center of the mountain. She looked up towards the sky. There could not be a reflection of the sun. Had she been hallucinating? Or is she hallucinating now?

"Do you see that?"

Jeremiah leaned over towards her window. "See what?"

"There's a beam of light. Back on that mountain down there."

He shook his head. "Probably reflection of sunlight against something. Maybe the ROVER?"

She shook her head. "No. The ROVER is too small. I don't know what that is."

She sat back in her seat.

But she knew.

And as the pod lifted higher into the darkness of space, and as the red planet became the sphere once again, she knew that she had discovered something down on the surface. Whatever the light source was, she felt it was coming from the surface, or the side of the mountain. She looked over at Jeremiah. He leaned back in his chair with his arms behind his head. He was clearly relaxing as the pod navigated towards the ship. She couldn't get the image of the empty suit out of her mind. And the three mounds.

Could they actually have been graves?

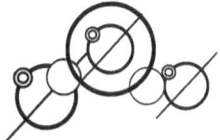

COUNSELOR ABAGAIL LOOKED OUT the pod window at the ship and gasped. "Is it truly that huge?"

Jeremiah looked over at her, nodded and smiled as he navigated the pod towards one of many receiving bays.

Her mouth hung open as she looked at the vast, cosmic cylinder. It had to be miles long. And the long cylinder rotated.

Slowly.

"That creates gravity," he said. "And the cylinder is so large, you don't notice the curvature inside."

She looked up at the soaring ship.

The cylinder was indeed rotating, and the windows were so small that she couldn't see anything inside.

"There are many observation decks," Jeremiah offered. "But everything is contained within the hull. Giant observation windows. Especially towards the central locations of the ship. There is a Town Square, and neighborhoods with houses, trees, cars. Shops and bars. Most of the thousands who are on this ship will be there for their entire lives."

"So it's like an arc."

Jeremiah nodded. "That's exactly what it's like. Full of the people who were rescued from Earth."

"And are there people back on Earth?"

Jeremiah looked at her and nodded as the doors to the receiving bay swung outwards. He eased the pod closer to the chamber. "They were given a choice. Free will to stay, or to come on the ship. Some came, others stayed."

As the pod eased to a stop in the center of the bay, she looked over at him as he released the controls. "How do you know so much about this ship?"

He removed his helmet and looked her in the eyes. "I just have had a blast exploring it! And I have been talking with those in white. That's the crew. They have told me quite a bit. They look like us, walk and talk like us, but they are from a different star constellation. And they rescue those who are on dying planets. Just like they did with us."

"I see," she said, following him out the door and down a set of metal steps which had been rolled up towards the side of the pod. Once she stepped out, her memory started to return. And at the base of the stairs, she gasped as she saw two familiar, loving faces.

"Winston! Eli!" she cried out as Jeremiah stood aside and let her run down the stairs. She opened her arms and the three of them hugged each other tightly. Eli was crying, and Winston patted her back.

"We are so happy to see you!" Winston said, leaning in close towards her ear. "You don't know how upset Eli has been lately. Once you slipped into that ravine, we had been certain you were gone. Your suit was no longer communicating. Did Jere tell you about how we celebrated when we received your call from the Red Outpost?"

She nodded and wiped some tears away from her cheeks. "Yes, he did. I can't believe I am seeing you guys again! But what about my vitals? You got nothing?"

Winston shook his head. "We received nothing, Abby. We were instructed from Vega One to complete the mission and they were working on putting together a mission to return to the surface and retrieve your body."

Counselor Abagail looked at Jeremiah. "I thought Copernicus was about to leave?"

He slowly nodded. "Yes…"

Her face shifted but then she focused back on Winston. "But then I contacted you."

Eli raised his eyes and looked up at her. "And then you contacted us. And I rejoiced!"

She smiled and hugged Eli close to her chest.

"You have always been a favorite of mine, Eli. You're always so sweet. How did you wind up with us?"

He smiled and wiped his eyes with his forearm. "I just fell into it. I mean, I've known Winston for years and years. But I remember Sector B very well."

"Sector B…" she said.

Jeremiah's footsteps clanked down the metal stairs. "Ok guys," he said. "Let's get back. Word is that we are going to be leaving the Martian system shortly and Copernicus and Moses want to meet with us. There is a new mission. Abby, you'll be taken to medical for clearance and the rest of us should go ahead and report."

Counselor Abagail released Eli and turned around to face Jeremiah. "A new mission? What are you talking about?"

"They will brief us after you have had a chance to rest."

Later, the team went to Town Square to let off some steam together. After showering and dressing in fresh clothes in each of their respective quarters, they met at the Borderline station.

In the vast clear hull on the opposite side of the tracks, Mars was still an imposing red sphere.

Counselor Abagail stood and leaned against the cool wall as the others chatted amongst themselves while waiting for the arrival of the tram. She looked at what appeared to be a giant crater on the side of the planet. She thought the planet looked fiery; if not angry. Why did the red planet appear so hostile?

Jeremiah noticed her deep in thought, staring at Mars, and leaned down in front of her, lining his face directly with hers. "That's where we were, Abby!" He turned around, eyes wide, leaning forward over the tracks, craning his neck forward.

"Utopia planitia," she said. "Yes, I remember."

Jeremiah turned around and beamed. "So you remember! Your memory is returning! Do you remember getting there yet?"

She shook her head and joined Jeremiah at the edge of the track. "So the edge of those dark mountains that surround the Red Outpost must be the edge of that crater?"

Winston joined them as the tram pulled forward. "Yes, that's exactly correct," he said.

As the tram accelerated towards the center of the ship, Abby leaned against the glass and watched the Red Planet.

She studied the crater.

Looked for the shining light. But no matter how hard she tried, she couldn't see it.

Had the light gone out?

The Borderline tram pulled up towards the Town Square Station with a slight hiss. As they exited, boisterous activity filled the area. Music wafted in from a bar towards the opposite end of the soaring atrium.

Counselor Abagail looked upwards. The atrium was lined with buildings and homes. Storefronts. There was a sky with light. Trees.

A lake.

It was filled with people.

Some dined at small sidewalk cafes. Others walked dogs through the park. She turned back towards the others. Her eyes were wide. "This is…unbelievable!"

Eli rushed forward and put his arm around her shoulders. They walked into the crowds, closer to the music – rock and roll; the drums were pounding out from a packed bar. He leaned close to her ear.

"Many of these people – if not all of them – will never see their destination. Those in white are making them as comfortable as possible for their journey. Because the journey is all that they have left."

She gasped.

"The journey will take so long, that many will have died out. Those in white – the Vegans – are making the survivors as comfortable as possible so they can enjoy the remainders of their lives. And so they reproduce."

She looked over towards the park. A little girl was walking a small puppy in a swath of sunlight.

"That little girl is a perfect example. By the time the ship reaches the Lyra constellation, she will be at the end of her life."

She looked upwards and saw what appeared to be a replica of the sun shining down on the vast, open area. "It's like the Earth was before the shift!"

Eli looked at her and nodded. "That was the point. The Vegans are hopeful that they saved enough of the human population to colonize a new planet."

They arrived at the bar with the loud, live rock music.

Most of the small tables which were scattered about the area were full, and there was no room at the bar. After a few minutes, Jeremiah approached one of the proprietors. The owner was one of the Vegans dressed in white. He looked over at them, and waved several other Vegans over.

They quickly bussed a dirty table, just on the side of the square where the team had entered from. The loudest of the music was muffled by a set of swinging doors so they could still engage in a conversation.

"So Abby, what do you remember?" Jeremiah asked as several tall, amber glasses of beer were served by a Vegan waitress at their table.

She leaned back and exhaled. And then shook her head slowly. "Not much…she said. I remember some but have blanks."

He nodded. "What's the *last* thing that you remember?" Winston and Eli looked at her, both taking sips of their beers.

Counselor Abagail looked into her glass. She saw the foam hugging the side, making the same circular pattern as the mountains around the crater on Mars.

She closed her eyes, and saw the dark ring of rocks.

The plateau that reached around the massive red dust bowl. And then she saw the scene in her mind: the same vision, looking through the sand-covered visor, hearing the howl of the winds.

"I woke up to my faceplate covered in sand. The winds were howling. I tried contacting each of you…but I received no answers."

Winston leaned forward.

"We were probably gone by then. We had to have been. If we were still on the surface, perhaps, we might have been in range to hear you."

Jeremiah placed his hand on Winston's arm. "No, no, Winston." He looked over at Abby. "We took your suit back with us from the Red Outpost. It's being tested now in the Research Lab. We are going to determine what happened to your communication system, Abby."

She shook her head.

"What is it?" Jeremiah asked.

She finished the last of the amber beer and placed her glass down on the table. She looked directly at Jeremiah as Winston and Eli looked on.

"It's the image that I can't get out of my mind, Jeremiah. It's the one that was the most striking. The one which I cannot understand, for the life of me."

"What was it?"

"Your suit. I saw your *empty* suit lying at the base of the ridge."

He shrugged. "I'm right here. And I didn't take my suit off. At least not down there. I wouldn't have survived five minutes!"

She sighed and shook her head. "I don't know, Jeremiah. I don't know how to explain it. I'm just so exhausted. I really need some rest."

Jeremiah nodded and Winston and Eli rose from their chairs.

"You might have been hallucinating," he said. "None of us know what really happened to you down there."

Abby got up, pushed her chair in, and nodded. "I'm heading back to my quarters, guys. I can barely keep my eyes open. So tomorrow is our new briefing?"

They all nodded in unison. "Yes. They have given us a new mission."

Abby smiled and nodded, turned and navigated the crowds back to the Borderline station. She folded her arms as she walked, and kept looking down. She saw what looked like grass. As the boisterous activity around her faded into the background, she knelt down, running her hand over the blades. She dug her fingers down and grabbed some dirt in her hand. As she reached back up, she opened her palm.

Dirt.

Blades of grass on a gigantic spaceship cruising through the galaxy.

Could she be imagining this?

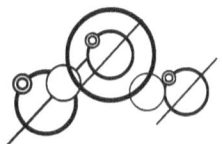

A ROTATING ENVELOPE appeared on the wall panel with an audible tone.

Counselor Abagail removed the needle from the side of her knee and placed the clear bag on the nightstand. She padded over to the panel and touched it with her finger. The envelope expanded and revealed a message.

TAKE TRAM TO LEVEL 27
CONFERENCE 3.5.2.2 FOR MISSION
BRIEFING.

The message flashed as she opened the side panel on the screen. A listing of photos of the others on her team cascaded down the side. She touched Jeremiah's photo and it expanded on the screen. After a few seconds, it was replaced with him live. He was rubbing his eyes. "Yes, Abby?"

"Did you see the message from Vega One?"

He shook his head and she saw his eyes divert towards the left. He pursed his lips as his eyes scanned right to left. He looked like he was reading a more significant message.

"Did you receive a different message?"

"No, Abby. I got the same message. To report to level 27. But I did get another message. A bit on the briefing on the mission."

"Why would they send that to you and not to me?"

Jeremiah shook his head. "I don't know, Abby. So are we meeting at the Broadline?"

Counselor Abagail sighed. "Yes, yes. Just give me a minute. I wasn't expecting such an urgent message."
They signed off and the screen went black.

She picked the IV bag up from the bedside table and finished draining her knees. When she removed the needle and placed it in a small, plastic receptacle on the bedside table, she held the bag, now full of fluid. She got up, walked across the room to a small opening on the wall which read "Deposit Fluid Here". She hesitated for a moment before waving her hand in front of the panel, which opened with a slight hiss.

Jeremiah stood with Winston and Eli in the corridor outside of her room. She stepped out as the door closed behind her. "I still can't get used to those sliding hydraulic doors," she said, as Jeremiah raised his eyebrows and approached her. "Look, we decided to stay at Town Square after you left. Be gentle with us." She looked confused. "I thought we were meeting at the Broadline?"

"Now that we're all here," he said, "Maybe we can all come into agreement on what our mission is?"

Winston's face shifted. "What do you mean, Jere? We're being briefed, right?"

He nodded. "Yes, we are. But I think they are holding something from us."

"I knew it," Eli said.

They all looked at Eli. He hung his head down towards the floor and shook his head back and forth.

Counselor Abagail reached out and touched his chin. "You knew it?"

Eli raised his eyes and looked directly at Counselor Abagail and nodded.

"How did you know?" she asked, lowering her hand.

Eli looked up at the others. His eyes were wide. A drip of sweat ran from his hairline down the side of his cheek. "Do you remember, back on Earth? In Sector B? When the scout came?"

Counselor Abagail placed her arm around Eli and lowered her head and made eye contact with him. "What about it, Eli?"

He raised his hands and covered his face. "You remember when the scout came?"

Counselor Abagail nodded.

There had been the period of amnesia after her time on Mars, which now had lifted, at least somewhat, and she remembered standing in front of a window in the outer receiving chamber of Sector B. She saw the dark shadow approaching through the brilliant sunlight; a wanderer who had collapsed in front of the hydraulic doors. "I remember him..." she said.

The others each nodded. Counselor Abagail nodded. "Yes. I remember now, quite well. He came to us out of the blue. I remember taking him in."

Eli looked up at Counselor Abagail as the others looked on. "But you didn't hear what he said to me."

"What did he say?" Jeremiah asked.

Eli took a deep breath and stood up straight. Counselor Abagail released her embrace, and all stood, watching Eli.

Eli bit his lower lip, and looked at the others. Winston smiled wanly. "Go ahead, Eli. What did he say to you?"

"He told me that only one of us would hold the key to the portal. That only one of us could advance."

Jeremiah scoffed. "Sounds like a bunch of nonsense to me."

"Discover the key," he said. "That was right before he passed out."

"Why are you just telling us this now?" Winston asked.

Counselor Abagail watched as Eli lowered his eyes and shook his head. "I didn't think anything of it at the time. I thought maybe he was delirious and suffering from radiation poisoning."

REPORT TO CONFERENCE 3.5.2.2. AT ONCE!

They all looked up as a dark, spherical drone hovered above them. Counselor Abagail leaned close to Eli and whispered in his ear. "We need to discuss this further. Later." Eli raised his eyes and looked up at her. His eyes were wide, pleading. She gave him a smile and gathered the group. "Let's go guys. They clearly are waiting for us. "

Conference Room 3.5.2.2. was located on the opposite end of the ship, and the four of them took the Broadline along the hull, and as the vast sea of stars passed on the clear side, she didn't look out at them this time. She looked at the others on her team. They all looked tired. And haggard. Eli and Winston sat on a small bench opposite where she had been standing. Jeremiah leaned against the wall, his eyes closed and his head leaning back.

She reached forward and snapped her fingers. "Hey!"

Jeremiah opened his eyes and looked back at her as Winston and Eli shifted on their bench. Jeremiah raised his eyebrows.

"How long did you guys stay at the pub last night?"

Jeremiah stretched his arms high above his head and yawned. "Just a few more…"

She looked over at Winston. He raised his eyebrows and shook his head.

"Are you guys for real?"

Jeremiah shrugged his shoulders, and stood. "Hey, I haven't had beer in eons. Back on Earth, we barely had enough water. Now, we have a Town Square with a bar that's at our disposal for no cost. Is it a crime that I like the amenities on this ship?"

She looked down and shook her head. As the tram pulled into the station, she looked up. "Are we all going to be okay for today's briefing?

As the door slid open, and Jeremiah walked out, he turned and looked down at her.

"We'll be fine Counselor."

They exited the tram in a soaring atrium.

This area was filled with all those in white. It did not have the crowds of Town Square, and it also did not have the grass, sidewalks, houses or buildings which dominated the square.

The atrium on this end of the ship was stark white. Further down Copernicus and Moses stood waiting under a large sign that read CONFERENCE.

As Counselor Abgail, Jeremiah, Winston and Eli approached, Copernicus extended his arms and smiled.

"Welcome, my team!" he beamed.

Moses reached up and placed his hand on Eli's shoulder and nodded. "Welcome everyone. Are you all well rested? We have much to discuss, and this is of the utmost importance. The fate of humanity is on the line now."

Counselor Abagail raised her eyes up towards Jeremiah. He shrugged. "We'll be fine," he said. "How far are we from 3.5.2.2?"

Moses looked at Jeremiah. "We are quite close. It's just in the bay of rooms back there."

Copernicus ushered everyone forward and towards the conference rooms. Once they were inside 3.5.2.2., he stood at the forward end of an expansive black table. Everyone found a seat as Copernicus stood at the end of the room with his hands clasped behind his back. He took a breath, closed his eyes and lowered his head for a moment.

After everyone was situated in a tall, leather chair, he looked at everyone. Moses sat in the front chair, looking up at him. Counselor

Abagail thought that Copernicus looked serious.

He placed his hands on the top edge of the front chair, and looked out at the team.

"One of my biggest fears I have is the failure of our mission," he said. He pulled the chair out and sat slowly, never breaking eye contact with each of the team. Counselor Abagail stared at him intently.

"It's unfortunate that the majority of the Earth survivors on this ship will not live to colonize the new planet. But the Vegan technology that allows for speed does not agree with the human body. Our physiology is different than yours and we are able to tolerate it.

Counselor Abagail remembered her astronomy studies from the University in the years before the shift back on Earth. "What about worm holes? I remember studying them. Are there any documented worm holes we could pass through?"

Copernicus raised his eyebrows and leaned back. "A very good question, Counselor. And Moses will explain to you some of the options regarding those phenomena."

Moses nodded and stood.

He walked to the front of the room and stood next to where Copernicus was sitting. He placed his hands on the back of his chair as Copernicus nodded in his direction and then returned to face the team. Counselor Abagail looked over towards Winston and Eli. Winston leaned forward and was watching Moses closely.

Eli was leaning back in his chair and his eyelids were drooping. She tore a piece of paper from the notepad in front of her seat and crumpled it. She tossed it at Eli who jumped when it hit him on the chest. He looked at her and shrugged his shoulders.

"Anything to add?" Moses looked at Eli, over towards Counselor Abagail, and back at Eli again.

Eli cleared his throat. "How is a worm hole going to get us anywhere? The ship is too big."

Moses smiled and raised his index finger. "Exactly!" he said. Copernicus grinned.

"We haven't the technology to create the negative matter to expand a worm hole."

Counselor Abagail straightened in her chair. "I've studied worm holes years ago. They are fleeting – sometimes only appearing for seconds at a time before closing. But they can be a straight shot to a distant galaxy if the negative antigravity can be created to keep the wormhole expanded and open for a ship to pass through."

"And we don't have that technology," Moses added.

"So why are we discussing it?" Winston asked.

"Because there are rumors of a portal," Copernicus said. "Beneath the icy surface of Europa. The portal opens a portal which resembles worm hole through which you can safely enter the constellation Lyra. As an individual, not a large ship."

Counselor Abagail raised her head and looked directly at Copernicus. "A portal? Interesting…"

"You mean so it *is* like a worm hole?" Jeremiah asked. "How would someone pass through without a ship?"

Copernicus shook his head.

"For this…not exactly," he said. He waved his hand back and forth over the black glass table. A graphic appeared – a blue tined icy sphere, etched with a network of orange tinted lines.

"It's a portal," Copernicus added. "It's similar to a worm hole, but still holds much mystery."

"Behold, Jupiter's moon Europa," he said. The graphic enlarged and zoomed in towards the surface. Counselor Abagail leaned forward, over the table and noticed that the orange lines actually appeared to be salt deposits and orange cosmic dust which blows off of Jupiter. Copernicus continued. "The surface remains blue and fresh, as the surface ice is warmer than the rest of the planet, and is constantly being recycled."

Counselor Abagail studied the hologram of the ice moon for a few minutes and then leaned back in her chair. "So you are saying there is a portal there? Where is it?"

Moses nodded and stood. "It's thought to be underneath the surface ice. Our beacons detect it in a certain cavern. But it's small and very inaccessible."

The graphic changed, as an image of a giant drill appeared, cylindrical, the size of a telephone pole.

"You see," Copernicus said, "we have to access it through a deep layer of surface ice."

The team nodded. "We used to study Europa years ago," Winston said. "We discovered an ocean under the ice."

Moses leaned over the table as the graphic depicted the drill driving through the surface ice and, as the ocean beneath is exposed from the chipped frozen pieces falling away, "Exactly!"

Jeremiah shook his head.

Copernicus looked at Jeremiah and raised his eyes. "What is it, Jeremiah?"

"So you have these massive drills and you say you can break through the surface ice, right?"

Moses and Copernicus both nodded. Winston and Eli leaned forward. Counselor Abagail leaned back in her chair and watched Jeremiah. He stood and moved around the table, standing next to Moses. "So we break through the surface ice," Jeremiah said. "And we find a super-massive ocean – which we won't know how deep it is – and where does it get us? Nowhere! Because you both reminded us that we don't have the technology to expand a worm hole enough with antigravity to allow a ship to pass through."

Counselor Abagail leaned forward and played with a pen. "And the worm hole would be inaccessible," she added. "In the middle of an ocean which we know next to nothing about?"

The room erupted in chatter.

Copernicus raised his hands. "Please...please...everyone. What we have discussed before applies here. Now that your amnesia has worn off, I am certain that you each remember back in Sector B in your area on Earth when Moses approached your colony. And he told you to trust."

Counselor Abagail slammed her fists on the table. "How can we trust when there is so much unknown?! We are the team you are planning to send there. What happens when something goes wrong? It happens to *us!*"

Copernicus stood and leaned forward on the table, his palms flat on the surface. "The choice is yours," he said. "But I urge you all – *we* urge you all – to make the right decision. A decision for humanity."

Jeremiah scoffed and shook his head. "But we haven't discussed the purpose! We find this portal you speak of, then what? We don't know if it's even accessible."

"That's where it becomes a leap of faith," Moses said.

"And you have the will to say no," Copernicus said. He stood and looked at each member of the team. They looked up at him as he spoke. "So that is our mission. We drill through the surface ice. We have an amphibian aquatic rover which you can submerge and search for the portal. But you each have some thinking to do. You each have a choice to make. We find this portal, we can save humanity. Think about all of those people – your human brothers and sisters – who cannot survive the journey to the Lyra constellation."

The team remained seated and silent.

"I ask each of you to make a decision. To give them a chance for survival. We can send them through the portal – if it exists. We have reason to believe that it does. And no, we cannot get the ship through the portal."

The graphic in the center of the table disappeared and the surface darkened. Jeremiah stretched.

"Now, go, get some rest," Moses said. "Take some time to eat. Think. For sixteen hours from now, we will need to begin the cryogenic process."

The team stood.

"Wait a minute," Counselor Abagail said. "Cryogenics?" She glanced over at Jeremiah and then back at Moses and Copernicus. "We have to go back under?"

Copernicus stood and joined Moses at the door. It slid open revealing a corridor teeming with activity. Those who were dressed in white rushed through. "We have addressed the issue, Counselor, and do not anticipate any amnesic effects this time. This meeting is over. Please meet us in Cryogenics in precisely sixteen hours if you choose to go."

He and Moses left.

The others joined Counselor Abagail and Jeremiah at the door.

They slowly walked into the hallway as a group of crewmembers rushed around them and continued down the corridor.

Counselor Abagail shook her head.

She bit her lower lip and her eyes were darting around the corridor, watching the crew. It seemed as though preparations were being made, and a rushed sense of urgency wafted through the crew area. She looked at the others as they stood silently. "When they told me that we had been cryogenically cooled in hyper-sleep for the trip to Mars I had no memory of it. The amnesia was so bad that I couldn't even remember who I was…or how I had gotten here."

"And what was the deal with having to drain our knees?" Eli asked.

Jeremiah shook his head and placed his hand on Counselor Abagail's shoulder. "Since this is such a mystery," he said, "Why don't we head over to Cryogenics and see for ourselves? I mean, if they want us to go back into stasis we need to see what we are dealing with."

The others nodded as Counselor Abagail leaned against the wall. She closed her eyes for a moment, and listened to the activity around them. As she blocked her sense of vision, she felt that her hearing became more acute. She could hear the rumble of the engines as the ship cruised the Martian system. And in her mind, she could see the fiery planet.

The Red Planet.

And on the surface, the three mounds that looked so much like graves. Jeremiah seemed to be acting more like himself, despite her earlier concerns in the receiving chamber.

Take a leap of faith...

Those words continued to ring through her mind like a metronome. How could she trust those around her...whether it be the Vegans, or now, even Jeremiah, who has chipped away at her confidence? There was just something different about everything.

Still, despite her reservations, Jeremiah was, in fact, behaving like himself. Winston and Eli, on the other hand, had been unusually quiet throughout the entire Europa briefing. There seemed to be something a little different about them, but they did have a traumatic experience on Mars themselves, especially when they thought she was lying dead at the bottom of a deep ravine.

Fall forward.

She took a breath, exhaled, and opened her eyes. Jeremiah was leaning his shoulder against the wall, looking right at her. He cracked a smile and raised his eyebrows. "So…to cryogenics?"

She looked at Winston and Eli who were standing and facing her. Both smiled.

She nodded. "Let's go check these hibernation pods out."

Still, with the transition to the preparation for the journey to Europa, she couldn't get the question out of her mind: what happened to her team on the surface of Mars?

Cryogenics was located throughout the ship in multiple satellite locations. Jeremiah led them through the corridors, turning around and gesturing for them to follow.

"Speed up guys! We can walk to this one!"

Counselor Abagail had to break into a walk-run to keep up. "Jeremiah!" she called. He turned and waved his hand forward but did not stop.

"You're moving so fast like you know the ship!"

He continued facing forward but she saw him nodding as charged ahead. "I do!" he said. "You wouldn't believe how much exploring I have done!"

After a few more minutes of navigating the busy corridors, Jeremiah approached a large set of doors. A sign read "CRYOGENICS" spanning the wall above the doors. The doors slid open, and a familiar male voice spoke before he had a chance to turn around.

"Hello Jeremiah. I thought you would be heading here."

The rest of the team caught up as Counselor Abagail caught her breath. The corridors looked the same as the other areas of the ship – long, polished steel flooring, stark white walls with networks of black panels with colorful; displays – but there was a lack of activity in this area.

"Moses!" Winston exclaimed. Counselor Abagail leaned against the wall and looked over at Moses. He was nodding and smiling.

"As I said, after our discussion in 3.5.2.2. I had a feeling that you would be seeking out Cryogenics." He extended his arm and placed it in the small of Jeremiah's back. "And Jeremiah here has taken many tours of the ship recently, so I knew he would know where this area was."

Jeremiah nodded.

"Well!" Moses said. "Let me show you the pods and how things will work when you are in Cryogenic stasis."

They filed into the main holding area.

Several medical personnel manned workstations in similar white dress as the other crew. But in this room, this area, the function was far more specialized.

In front of the far wall was a line of rectangular pods. Long, rectangular chambers with clear covers. Just large enough to hold an average sized person. Each pod was closed, and roughly one and a half feet wide by approximately six feet long, sitting on a permanent slab raising it several feet above the floor.

Counselor Abagail hadn't realized she had been holding her breath while they were slowly walking closer to the hibernation chambers. She exhaled. "Moses," she said.

He looked at her and smiled. "Yes?"

"What makes you think that we can survive this?"

"Because you already have."

Jeremiah scowled. "Now let me get this straight," he said, looking up and over at Moses. "You mean to tell me that we will be frozen for the duration of this journey?"

Moses leaned over one of the pods and shook his head as the others looked on.

"No, no. You will be in stasis. In a cryogenic stasis chamber on Deck D. Everyone who has been selected for this journey from your planet has been selected for a specific reason. There are several exoplanets in the Lyra constellation that can be suitable for your population – but in order to get there, this is a necessary step."

Counselor Abagail rose to her feet. Her face shifted and her face was awash with concern. "Cryogenics? Like inducing hypothermia?"

"That's precisely what it means," Moses said. "You will each be submerged in a highly oxygenated, super cooled breathing fluid. Your vital signs will be closely monitored. Once the chamber fills with the fluid and it covers your face, you will be instructed to take the fluid into your lungs and begin breathing normally."

Winston, Jeremiah and Eli looked at each other.

This was sounding familiar.

"We dove under the ocean back on Earth with a highly oxygenated perfluorocarbon fluid," Jeremiah said. "We submersed in pressure bubbles that filled with the fluid."

"Yes, we know," Moses said. "That is one of the reasons why you have been selected for this purpose. We have chosen you for this mission to Europa because we have the drill and the equipment. Now that we have you, we have the manpower with the skill set."

They met in the outer chamber as the ship PA system announced departure in T-minus 30 minutes.

"But this is a different fluid than what you experienced in your deep sea exploration," he continued. "This is super cooling. Your body will be cooled to 32 degrees Celsius."

Jeremiah lifted his eyes and turned his head toward Nelson as the others looked on. "You're telling us this again, I would assume. I still cannot remember anything about the journey from Earth to Mars, but am I correct in assuming that this was the same fluid that we were submerged in for that journey?"

Moses nodded.

Jeremiah scoffed. "So you're saying that when we wake we'll have to go through this again? The amnesia?" He shook his head and gave an exasperated sigh.

"We have been working on the side effects of the technology for your kind," Moses said. "We are confident that we won't have that error this time around."

Counselor Abagail looked down at the cryogenic chamber as the fluid filled and the lid lowered. "And what happens if something goes wrong? Like a medical emergency or something? Who will save us?"

Moses nodded. "Understandable concern. You will be monitored closely. For the first several years of the mission, we – the crew – will have rolling periods of stasis."

"Rolling periods?" Counselor Abagail asked.

Moses nodded.

"Only certain segments of the crew will be in stasis for a set amount of time," he explained.

"And then that group is awakened, and the next group enters hibernation. It will roll that way for the first several years, and then, for the latter half of the journey, the ship will operate on its own and all essential crew will be under stasis. Only certain specific crewmembers will be kept awake to tend to the survivors needs."

"I hate being submerged," Eli said, removing his suit.

"So let me get this right. The liquid keeps us preserved and unaged as we head towards the Jovian system," Jeremiah said. "At the speed they have us cruising, it's going to take years to get there. What about our muscular definition? Will we wake up as vegetables? Will our muscles have turned to mush?"

The doors on the other side of the chamber slid open with a hiss as everyone turned their heads.

Copernicus walked over to them and stood next to the sample pod. He raised his eyes directly to Jeremiah. "We have addressed that technology concern already."

Counselor Abagail stepped closer to the pod and looked over at Copernicus. "Jeremiah raises a valid concern." She looked at Jeremiah and then Winston and Eli. Winston nodded in agreement as Eli bit his lower lip. She turned to Copernicus.

"What has been done?"

"The muscles are stimulated while in hibernation," Copernicus said. "It's actually a technology that has been in place for quite some time. And as we said before, each of you has already been in cryogenic stasis before."

The team returned to their shared common quarters just off BAY 1. They stood together in the small locker room where they would dress and prepare for their missions. Counselor Abagail leaned against the cool metal and looked out into the hanger where MACA 1 was parked and secured, its sleek, black nose pointed out towards the massive hydraulic doors.

"We could just get in there and go back to Mars," she said.

Eli scoffed and tossed his radiation suit on the floor. He threw his boots to the other side of the room and they clanked against the steel. "Why are we even going?"

Counselor Abagail watched his interaction and pursed her lips. She folded her undergarments and reached into her locker for a fresh sachet. She snapped it around her chest and pulled her hair back and tied it behind her head. "You were listening in the briefing, right?"

Winston and Jeremiah both looked at her with blank stares on their faces. Eli was sitting on the floor next to his piled uniforms and looked up at her.

"When we arrive at Europa, we're going to excavate through the ice," she said. "Moses said they have these things called cryobots that we can release remotely from the ship here and it will melt the ice beneath the surface. What we find after that is – "

" – is the unknown," Jeremiah added.

Counselor Abagail nodded as Winston helped Eli fold his clothes.

"We plan to melt through the surface cracks," Winston said. "But we have to hibernate. We can't return to Mars.

Jeremiah shook his head. "Do they even know what's there?" His face shifted. "They claim there's this portal. But how do they know?"

"They don't," Winston said. "But the only way to find it is to go there. And go into cryogenics. They say they fixed the amnesia problem."

"And we have to trust them," Eli said. "That's what they said."

Counselor Abagail sighed and kept staring at MACA1. "It's our leap of faith," she said quietly.

Jeremiah and Winston turned over to face her. "What did you say?" Jeremiah asked.

She turned around and looked at the other three members of her team. "A leap of faith.

They have been asking me to trust. All we can do is just that. If we want to be a part of this mission. Remember what Moses has always said. We have free will to choose not to be a part of this."

Eli stood. "Why do we need to locate this portal anyway?"

Winston looked over and faced Eli. "I visited with the crew and I saw the research and the data they collected over years. There are indicators of a portal to the Vegan star system. Like a tiny worm hole. Difficult to access, as you can see. By shuttling the survivors down to and through the portal, and having them enter through that way, they have a chance of survival on the new, habitable planet, as opposed to living their lives out on the ship just trying to get there."

"They can't be placed into stasis too?" Eli asked.

"The ship isn't equipped to handle that," Jeremiah said. "There are only pods for the crew plus a small percentage. This is designed to be a passenger vessel. And the journey to Vega will take far longer than a human lifetime."

"I think they're just as clueless as we are," Jeremiah said. "So they harnessed antimatter. Great. Just dandy. So we can get to Vega. But it's still going to take longer than a human lifetime. And then we have this Europa idea...no one even *knows* what's under the ice anyway. It's a moon that's had little exploration and even less in recent years. How does *anyone* even know if this isn't just an extraordinary waste of time and resources?"

Counselor Abagail raised her hands. "Now, Jeremiah. This is our mission. That is our goal. This is our purpose. You can choose to rebel, as I recall you did back on Earth with Elder Cane. But now, things are different. We don't even know if we have an Earth to go back to. And Moses and his kind have the ability to save our race. Our human race. We don't *know* if there is a portal there. But we *believe* that there is. Their data indicates that it leads to the exoplanet that the Vegans are populating. But none of the data is exact. It's still a mystery. We just don't know until we excavate and explore."

Jeremiah leaned back on the lockers and shook his head.

"That's the part that's the leap of faith," she said. "We have an opportunity here to save thousands of lives. Yes, they will be at least a decade older once we arrive at Europa than they are now. But if the portal is there…we can get them to Vega. They can live."

Jeremiah nodded.

"And yes, there is that small seed of doubt in my mind," she said. "About the amnesia. I feel it too. But like Moses said, we have to trust. They said they addressed the issue with cryogenics."

Eli sat on the small wooden bench that was fixed between the lockers. "It took me forever to even remember anything beyond this ship. What I'm afraid of is waking up several years from now – deeper in space – and being the same way we were when we approached Mars. I couldn't remember anything! It's like my mind was…washed. Clean."

Counselor Abagail raised her hands up. "Eli. We all had the same issue. We have the chance to be a part of something great here." She looked at each of them. "Are you guys in? Will you come to Europa with me?"

They each looked at her, and she paused and held eye contact with each of them.

After a few minutes, Winston finally spoke. "Then let's get going. If we're going to do this,

I want to see what's in that ocean underneath the ice."

Counselor Abagail smiled and nodded, and then looked over at Jeremiah, raising her eyebrows.

"I'm in," he said. "You know I'm not going to let you go alone. We're a team, girl."

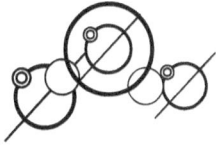

THERE WERE THREE METHODIC TONES from behind them. They turned and saw a small, spherical drone, hovering just a few feet from their faces. A tiny red light on the side flashed and in a small screen in the center of the sphere flashed a message in white block lettering:

READY WALTER DE JESUS ABAGAIL WINSTON

Counselor Abagail felt her stomach shift into knots. She looked up at Jeremiah who leaned towards her.

Eli looked up at Counselor Abagail as the drone patiently waiting at the entry to the locker chamber. He bit his lower lip. "It's just like what we breathed back on Earth. Isn't it? When we breathed the fluid underwater?"'

She shook her head slowly. "No…it isn't, Eli. You were still conscious in that breathing fluid. This here is totally different. This is going to render us unconscious and induce hypothermia."

Jeremiah sighed and nodded. "They know what they are doing."

She looked back at Jeremiah, who turned to follow the drone, along with Eli and Winston. They all had already stripped to their underwear, leaving their clothing in the lockers. She took a deep breath and sighed.

And as they followed the drone through the cold steel corridors, through the curve of the hull, she kept watching Jeremiah walk before her. He was brave. She would give him that.

But she knew, deep inside, that Jeremiah was just as uncertain as she was.

The drone rotated in front of them, leading the way down a network of corridors, most were windowless, doors were scattered throughout, and all were closed. They followed the sphere, as it hovered to the left, into a soaring atrium with the sign that read:

HYPERSLEEP PREPARATION AREA.

Others were in the waiting area, some sitting and chatting quietly

As they entered the hyper sleep chamber, Counselor Abagail faced Jeremiah, Eli and Winston. They looked at her, saying nothing, their faces expressionless, waiting in solitude.

She took a quick breath and released it. "Here we are, gentlemen. You are three brave men. The only three men that I have come to know on this ship. I still don't know where the others have vanished to. But now, we are at a precipice. Like you three did back on Earth, we must now, together take a leap of faith. We have to trust Moses and the others that they *do* know what they are doing, as you had said Jeremiah."

He nodded.

"And it's okay to be scared," she said. "I know you are three very tough men. But I won't think anything less of you if you show the emotions I know you are feeling inside. Because I am feeling them too."

Winston nodded to her with a faint smile. But it was Eli who spoke first.

"I…" he said. There was a quiver in his voice. "I…don't want to do this…" He looked over at Winston, shaking his head. "They can't make me do this! I can't…I don't want to die!" He reached up and wiped a tear from his cheek. Winston put his arm around his back and Jeremiah turned to face Eli. Counselor Abagail raised her hand, and gestured at Eli. "You are not going to die," she said. She placed her hand on his shoulder and spoke close to his ear. "This is sleep. Hibernation. Deep sleep, Eli. You will still be alive. And when you wake up, we will be in the vicinity of Jupiter. Do you remember looking at the maps of the solar system when you were a kid?"

He turned to face her and nodded. "I do remember. I remember seeing Mars from the telescope my Dad bought me for Christmas. But Jupiter…I have only seen from drawings and in books."

"And so we are just going from one point on that map to the other," she said. "When you close your eyes here, the next thing you will remember is waking up. You won't remember anything in-between."

"These look like coffins," Jeremiah said as the team entered Cryogenic Chamber 17. Counselor Abagail looked up at him and glared. Jeremiah shrugged his shoulders. "Well, they do."

Moses stood in front of the first row of cryogenic chambers, patiently waiting with a smile on his face. He was wearing a white coat and holding a clipboard. Several other medical staff surrounded him and prepped monitors medical items.

"Oh, they are not coffins, Mr. Walter. They are of the latest technology," Moses said, showing Counselor Abagail, Winston and Eli to the changing area. "Think of these as immortality pods. When you are awakened, you will not have aged even a minute…but years will have passed. Please undress to minimal clothing. A nurse will give you an antimicrobial soap to wash with, as well as a sterilizing rinse."

Eli unwrapped a fresh bar of bright green soap as Jeremiah grabbed Nelson's arm as he turned around. "You're saying we will not have aged at all when we wake up?"

Nelson shook his head. "Not one minute, Jeremiah. This ship is far too massive to operate on its own, despite having the technology to do so. As a precaution, we are initiating a rolling stasis. There will always be crew and medical staff alert at all times for the first half of the journey. During the second half, only certain crew and medical staff will roll through stasis."

Counselor Abagail "What about the others? The survivors? All those we saw in the Town Square. What about them?"

Moses looked at Counselor Abagail. "This technology is not available for everyone. Because the four of you are so important to the preservation of your kind, you will be held, ageless. Think of it as a gift. For the others, when we reach the Jovian system, the survivors will have aged nearly a decade."

Counselor Abagail stood naked in front of her team. She watched them. Winston stood behind his pod. He was quite muscular and strong. Eli was much smaller than he, and far more demure. He clasped his hands over his genitals and his cheeks were flushed. Jeremiah, on the other hand, was openly walking throughout the chamber, studying the monitors without regard for his nudity.

There was something about them. They had seemed so foreign, over time and then throughout the mind exploration, but now, even with her continued reservation, she felt that her team was her family.

She watched Jeremiah's tight buttocks flex as he leaned forward, moved and studied each panel. She laughed and shook her head.

He turned around, his eyes wide.

The doors slid open.

A team of those in white surrounded Copernicus.

"The ship is about to go on lockdown," he said. "The center regions of the ship are sealed off, and the four of you need to get into your pods. The medical team here will connect you to your vitals monitoring systems, and get you situated for your hyper sleep."

Eli's eyes widened and he snapped his head towards Winston. "I don't think I can do this…"

Winston placed his arms around Eli. "It's just like the pressure bubbles back on Earth. Do you remember how worked up you got when the fluid started filling the bubble?"

He wiped under his eyes and nodded. "Yes I do. But it was so hard to breathe! So heavy!"

Jeremiah grabbed Copernicus' shoulder. "How is this going to feel? Is Eli going to have a difficult time breathing?"

Copernicus shook his head as Counselor Abagail eased herself into her pod. She sat with her arms draped over her knees as Jeremiah stood between Winston, Eli and Copernicus.

"How is he going to *feel?*"

"There is no reason to panic," Copernicus said. Eli's eyes were wide. He covered his face with his hands and wiped his cheeks. Counselor Abagail tapped her hand on the side of her pod.

"Eli!"

He dropped his arms to his side and looked over at her. He had the big, droopy, sad eyes that she always remembered. "I'm going to be lying here right next to you. Just do what they tell you. It'll be okay."

Eli shook his head and eased himself into his pod, as Jeremey and Winston settled into the remaining chambers.

Several of the medical personnel visited each pod and connected tubes and wires to each of them. As they did, the black screens on the far wall sprung to life. "Please everyone lie flat on your backs, with your arms at your sides, and relax as best you can."

Counselor Abagail felt a chill in the bottom of the pod. It was the cool feeling of steel and was getting colder.

And then she closed her eyes.

She could hear Eli crying out, begging to be released from the chamber. She could hear Winston and Jeremiah consoling him; she even heard her own voice in an attempt to speak in a reassuring tone. But even for herself, there was the twinge of anxiety.

Of a knot in the stomach.

And the feeling of her heart racing in her chest as she felt the first drops of fluid underneath her back. She opened her eyes and tilted her head downwards. The fluid was building up fast, it was nearly an inch deep already.

She heard Copernicus in the room, speaking to the medical personnel. "Eyes closed! No talking. The fluid will cover and submerge you completely. When it does, breathe in."

Her back was numb.

And then her arms and legs. As the fluid built up in the pod, she gradually numbed, until she was stabilized and unable to move. She opened her eyes, peered down and saw the fluid level creep up her neck, towards her chin. She instinctively closed her mouth tight, drawing her lips together tight, as the fluid level covered her nostrils.

Her eyes darted from right…to left…and back.

"Eyes closed!"

But she did not listen.

And the room blurred as the fluid covered her completely. There was a deep rumble as the lid lowered over her, slowly, methodically; and as she recognized Copernicus standing over her pod, she saw a snippet of his white hair as the gap between the lid and the base grew smaller…until it was closed.

And then she opened her eyes.

As she looked downwards, she could see the pods. Four rectangular hibernation chambers. Each pod was connected with a network of wires and tubing towards a series of screens. Each screen had a photo and their last name. And as she moved closer to the pod that said "Abagail", she saw herself…but was that really her?

It was a person.

A life contained inside a closed pod; which did look like a coffin. She floated down towards the lid; the long viewing windows – glass rectangles that spanned the length of the chamber, from head to foot, were partially covered with ice crystals. And she saw the ice inside.

But the dark silhouette contained a life.

A person.

A life.

Had it really been her?

She floated upwards and towards the left. She could see the silhouettes in the other three pods.

Were they floating also?

She saw the room, up from afar, and there were no medical personnel. She could hear beeps and monitors, but the ship was otherwise silent.

She glided across the chamber towards the corridor. The doors did not slide open, but she floated through them effortlessly, into a stark and silent corridor. The hum of the engines was still there; but all activity had ceased.

She glided down towards a soaring atrium and clear side hull painting a star scape; tiny white sphere on a dark, black pallet.

And then she saw a plume, a soaring tail, crystal white outbursts; and the gigantic rock. Just on the edge of the hull. A complete blackout of the star scape; could she do it? Could she travel through the hull like she had through the doors to the hibernation chamber?

She floated forward.

And a bright flash.

And she was floating in a sea of tiny, white stars.

The little spheres reached outwards through eternity, and as she turned around, she saw the imposing giant floating rock; its long, white gaseous tail trailing outwards like a tentacle.

You are called on to be a leader.

The voice spoke to her, but she was alone.

She closed her eyes but continued to see.

She saw she was floating through the stars. They were tiny, pinpoint spheres, in all directions, surrounding her like a blanket of tiny lights against a dark palette; and as she levitated, she saw she was alone. And she could still remember. She no longer saw the icy fluid overtake her like a layer of clear, liquid plastic. It was Moses who had clearly been standing over her, watching her through the shimmery fluid as she felt a fuzziness move through her veins; a numbness overtake her mind. It hadn't been Copernicus watching her, had it? But now, she was floating, free, surrounded by her celestial orchestra. Had she fallen asleep? Was she now in hibernation? Was this a dream? Or was she dead?

She saw something in the distance.

A beacon of light.

And she immediately felt love, and hope. Something that overtook her being as the light drew nearer; but still, it appeared so far away, that it might have been in the outer reaches of the solar system.

But where was she?

She looked downwards but saw nothing; no physical body. She turned and faced behind her and saw, in the great, vast distance, the light of the sun. But the cosmic radiation did not harm her. And she imagined that Earth, the old and familiar home, as it once was, had been there; a small, spherical shadow in the foreground of the glowing light. Yes, she had been there. Her home for most of her life. The mother she had for most of her days when she had felt the sand between her toes; when she had listened to the dull roar of the surf, the pleasant, calming, soothing sound. She could still feel the winds on her face.

But that was the past.

And there, as she floated through the cosmos, there was no wind. In the cosmos there were no sounds; just merely silence. It painted a similar kind of beauty; the Earth was a mere cosmic bit of the vast masterpiece; the cosmos was colorful and creative; expansive and principled. It only spoke the truth through its impenetrable silence. But was it alive? Were the brilliant gas explosions heard...if no one were there to hear them? Were the planets and the star systems actually teeming with life? Had the molten rivers of Venus once been filled with water? Or were the desolate barren rocks of Mars...simply rocks?

She knew the Earth was that small, dark sphere in the foreground.

The sun shined brightly behind it. And she knew she was too far away to travel to it.

Was she?

The power is within.

She raised her head and looked behind her. There was a star, near to her, but at a distance which she could not determine. It was not like any of the other stars in the vast, infinite blackness.

This star was indeed different.

It was unique and bright; brighter than the countless other stars which surrounded it. But that particular star had soaring outbursts emanating from a white, hot sphere.

Trust yourself, Abby. And all will fall into place.

The giant asteroid blocked her view of the ship.

But ahead she saw her vision of the star; so bright, so warm, so vivid. She tried to open her mouth but nothing would come out.

The star moved closer and her voice cracked.

"Am I…dead…?"

She looked at the star. Muted colors swirled in the center of the pulsating whites and yellows, and she waited for an answer.

You are who you choose to be.

"Is there a portal underneath the ice of Europa?"

The star did not answer.

And she turned once again and the ship was still near. The long, rotating cylinder ahead of her. The star was far, off in the distance. And behind her, a round, dark, black star, surrounded by fingers of light. Had she traveled to the celestial landscape of destiny?

But she knew where she was destined for.

And through her mind, when she saw so many snippets of her life of what it once had been, they seemed so distant.

So unfamiliar.

For the cosmos, to her, felt like home.

The painted pastels; soaring gases, distant stars. And her journey, for which it was defined.

The Ice Moon.

3

MISSION: ICE MOON

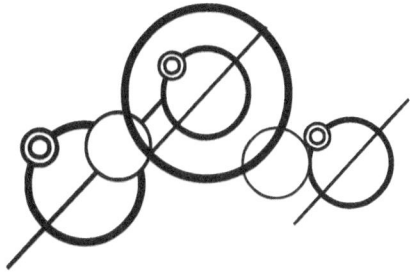

HER EYES OPENED as the light filtered into the chamber. The ice had melted, the liquid had heated, and she was warm. The lid then opened with the slight hiss of hydraulics. Had they arrived in the Jovian system? As the fluid drained, she slowly sat up. She reached out and grabbed the edges of the pod.

There was an alarm sounding.

The doors slid open.

She recognized Moses as he stormed into the room. "Get up, each of you!" He looked over at the medical staff who had been assisting each of the team members from their pods. "Reacclimatize them right away! We need them immediately!"

Counselor Abagail grabbed the sides of the pod and drew her knees up to her chest. Her eyes widened. "Moses…"

He shook his head as he was about to turn back to the corridor. "Reacclimatize, get dressed and join us on the bridge right away. We've been adrift. And have sustained damage. We must get back on course. Go! Now!"

He turned and ran down the corridor as the doors slid closed. Counselor Abagail looked over towards the other team members and saw Jeremiah sitting in his pod with his face buried in his hands.

"Jere!" she called. "You ok?"

He waved an arm. "Yeah…yeah…just a bit of a hyper sleep hang over."

She shook her head, and saw Winston and Eli with similar effects. She turned her attention to the scurrying medical personnel. One woman was examining her screen when Counselor Abagail called out. The woman turned to face her with an expressionless look.

"Have we been awakened early? How long have we been in stasis?"

The woman turned and touched the screen behind her pod several times, and then turned back to face Counselor Abagail.

"Forty-seven equivalent Earth years."

She took a breath and held it. Her eyes widened.

She looked over at Jeremiah.

"Jere!"

He was hoisting himself out of his pod, his back turned.

She found her voice and was louder, more insistent. "Jere!"

As he spilled on the floor, he grabbed the edge of his pod and held himself up. He opened his eyes and looked over at her.

Counselor Abagail slapped the sides of her pod. "We've been under for almost fifty years!"

She looked over at Winston and Eli. "Winston!"

Winston's mouth dropped open. "We've been under for almost fifty years!?"

Jeremiah nodded. "I heard. We're getting dressed and heading to meet Moses at the bridge."

They met in the corridor in crisp, stark white uniforms as the alarm sounded above. It was a short, harsh tone, sounding every few seconds, repeatedly. The Vegans were rushing through the corridors in haphazard directions. Counselor Abagail turned to the medical staff. The same woman who had checked her vitals smiled and nodded to her. "The bridge is forward." She gestured behind where Counselor Abagail was standing, down a stretch of corridor.

"Do you know what happened?" Eli asked.

She nodded.

"We were knocked off course by an asteroid shower and have been drifting out of the galaxy."

Counselor Abagail let out a gasp.

The image of the asteroid flashed through her mind. Had she been dreaming? Predicting a future? Or witnessing what was happening? She turned to the crew member. "Weren't crew members monitoring this? I thought Moses and Copernicus talked about a rolling stasis? Was the ship left unmonitored?"

She shook her head. "That is all I know, I'm sorry."

Counselor Abagail nodded and looked at the team. "Winston, you've been to the bridge before, right?"

He nodded.

"Okay then, take the lead. Get us there. We'll follow you. We have to talk to Copernicus and find out what happened."

The corridors heading to the bridge were wide and teeming with activity.

A bay of several steel sliding doors opened and revealed a network of terminals with Vegans in white staffing them. To the left was a large, circular command station. Copernicus was standing in the center, looking outwards, unaware of their presence. Counselor Abagail looked to the right. There was a soaring view of the star scape, and a black circle in the distance.

And then she thought of her dream.

She gasped.

"Copernicus!"

He looked over and rushed down to them. He waved his arm as Moses looked up from an exterior station and joined them.

Before Counselor Abagail could speak, Winston took a deep breath and released it. He leaned forward, looking directly at Copernicus. "What happened?"

Copernicus was watching out through the windows intently. "Take a look at Gensys 1," he said.

They looked outwards and saw a swirling ring of light surrounding a sphere of complete blackness. Copernicus continued.

"We'd studied this in the past. She's got us in her grip…"

"A black hole?" Counselor Abagail stepped closer to the windows. "How is that even possible?"

He shook his head. "I'll explain later." He pointed to the black sphere. "You see that? We're in its gravitational pull. I've tried back thrusters. Everything. It's sucking us in."

Winston walked towards the windows. "It's a black hole. We're not being sucked in. We're *falling*." He turned to face the others, his hands on his hips. "Copernicus! Have your crew move hard port at max power. Stay on the edge. How did we get to this point?" He raised his eyebrows and looked at Copernicus and Moses.

The alarm continued its urgency above.

Counselor Abagail looked at Copernicus and then over at Moses with wide eyes. "What is the plan?"

Winston cleared his throat. "We can move around it," he said. "We must go at an angle. It will take all the ship's power. But it can be done."

Counselor Abagail looked up at Winston. "Are you sure?"

As Winston spoke, and explained the theory behind supermassive black holes, she looked out into space. Her mouth dropped open.

There it was.

A ring of light, pulling light into it, soaring inwards to pure blackness. Gaseous light, reaching out towards the ship.

The bridge shook and she held onto a beam. She turned around as the others slowly got to their feet. Winston charged the circular command station.

"If we remain on direct course we will be vaporized!" he said, leaning over the station. Jeremiah and Copernicus joined Winston.

Jeremiah leaned close to Copernicus. "If we remain on the edge, like Winston says, where will this put us?"

Copernicus turned to the crew lining the back wall. "We must find the worm hole we entered through! Send coordinates!"

The ship rumbled and shook again as Counselor Abagail steadied herself. After the turbulence subsided, she joined the others at the command station.

A graphic superimposed itself over the viewing area and all eyes were trained on it. On the edge of the black sphere the gridlines curved inwards.

"There's a wormhole over there!" Moses exclaimed.

Copernicus stood behind a high captain's chair as the ship rumbled. "Set coordinates and arrival estimate. And get us out of this pull!" he said. The alarm sounded and the lights flashed.

Winston remained standing and held onto the command station. "It's not pulling us we are falling! We can steer around this!" He looked back at Copernicus with wide eyes. "Can you get us through the wormhole?"

Copernicus nodded. "We've already been through it. We have to return. The key is to *find* it…"

Counselor Abagail nodded. "Go through the worm hole. That's our only course back."

Copernicus issued his command: "Map it. Where will the worm hole take us?"

The graphic zoomed as the crew members sitting at the command station swiveled around in their chairs. All were watching them as the lead crew member analyzed the incoming data. "The worm hole should bring us back to the Milky Way – if it's still open and in the same place. This one appears to be moving. According to saved data, Vega One veered off course just beyond the Jovian system after being assaulted by a field of giant asteroids. The communication system was damaged and severe damage was sustained in the central areas of the ship. The ship was placed on course with the worm hole and entered right through it."

Moses raised his head and looked up at the others. "Town Square is destroyed. The ship sealed itself immediately after impact."

Counselor Abagail looked over at Moses. "What about the people? The survivors?"

Moses looked at her and shook his head.

Jeremiah slammed his palms on the console. "How could this have happened?! What happened to monitoring and rolling stasis?!"

"We *did* have a rolling stasis of the crew, as planned," Copernicus said. "Something happened that we cannot currently explain! It seems we were all either sleeping or unconscious. But we have been adrift in this uncharted galaxy for forty seven *years*! And I have no means to explain it other than the passage of time in this galaxy is far different than the Milky Way. All I can do is go on the data from Vega One to attempt to find the worm hole and get us back to the Jovian system."

Jeremiah shook his head and crossed his arms as the Vega One shook violently. They all fell to the floor as Eli hit his head on the edge of the console. Winston crawled over to Eli and shouted in his ear. "Eli! You okay?!"

"Get us around this pull!" Copernicus shouted. "She's tearing us apart!"

The hull rumbled and creaked as Counselor Abagail raised her head and looked out at Gensys 1.

"Why, hello there, little star…"

She saw the pin point of light. It shot outwards from the heart of the darkness, out towards the ship.

Take the leap of faith, Abby.

The rings of gaseous light swirled around the dark sphere, and as she looked closer towards it, she saw the light bend upwards…and outwards…over…and under…swirling light fingered outwards.

Trust yourself.

The ship shook violently as she turned around to face the others. All were lying on the floor as the crew initiated overhead safety harnesses. Eli turned his head and looked over at her. His eyes were wide and his face painted with fear. "We're going to make it," she said. She reached over and held his hand as he bit his lower lip and closed his eyes. She crawled closer to him. "The worm hole is just beyond the black hole." She spoke softly, just next to his ear. "Everything is going to be all right. We will find the worm hole right where the graphics say it is and will be back on the mission soon. And everything will be *just fine…*"

The hull creaked and they raised their eyes upwards.

"Hard port!" Copernicus said. He grabbed the edge of the console and held tight. "Full power!"

"We are at full power Captain!"

Counselor Abagail put her arm around Eli and turned her head to face the window as the bridge filled with bright light.

Vega One shook and rumbled as the light was blinding and she closed her eyes.

She listened. She could hear Copernicus speaking to himself, over and over.

"Hold together, hold together, hold together…"

And then she heard Eli's voice. "Are we going to make it through, Abby?"

And the rumble became deafening as Counselor Abagail and Eli were knocked apart. She was flung towards the windows and rolled against the side of a console.

And then the shaking and deafening roars abated.

They could hear the urgency of the alarm again. Counselor Abagail opened her eyes and saw the crew adjust their harnesses. Copernicus grabbed the side of the command station and hoisted himself up. "Status update."

The crew members studied the panels for a moment as the ship leveled out.

"Central sector seal held. Hull breach in sectors 51 and 53 and were sealed. Otherwise we are intact."

He let out a deep breath and looked over towards the others. "Jeremiah, Abby. We've made it."

Winston eased himself up onto his elbows as Eli was crying softly, his arm draped over his eyes.

Counselor Abagail joined Copernicus at the command station as Jeremiah joined them as well. "Copernicus," she said. "I don't think we will have to spend too much time looking for the worm hole. I am confident it's in the same spot as where we entered through it."

He nodded but Jeremiah spoke. "But the navigation system was damaged, wasn't it?"

"We will have to search for it manually," Winston said from the floor. He was still comforting Eli. "Look for curvature in the star pallet."

"Curvature?" Jeremiah asked.

"A worm hole is where space time bends inwards and creates a hole – a shortcut to a distant galaxy," Copernicus said.

"And are they easy to find?" Counselor Abagail asked.

"That depends," Winston said.

Copernicus walked over to Winston and Eli. "I have crew sounding the ship. So it's safe to take him to medical. When we go through the worm hole, it'll get rough again, but nothing like we just experienced."

"I'll stay here," Counselor Abagail said. "I am confident I will find this worm hole."

Copernicus nodded at her and turned. "Moses! Please accompany Winston and Eli to medical. And I will make an announcement when we are approaching the worm hole for everyone to strap in."

Moses nodded and assisted Winston with Eli. Counselor Abagail approached Jeremiah and placed her hand on his arm. "Are you staying up here with us?"

Bridge activity returned to normal around them as the crew scanned for the worm hole.

He nodded.

"I can help you, Abby. I've been through this before. This searching through space. So many things that happened back on Earth that everyone thought I was hallucinating."

"I didn't believe you were," she said.

They both stared out into the star scape. "There's something about it," he said. "Some cosmic connection. I don't know why the star chose *me*, but it did. It's like it spoke to me. Every time I closed my eyes, I would see the star."

"I think I am having similar visions."

He looked at her and raised his eyebrows. "Do tell."

"Well, when we were supposedly in stasis, I had what I *thought* was a dream. And I was floating above our hibernation pods. At first, I thought I had died. That I'd somehow not survived the hypothermic cooling procedure. I was floating in the room, and then I could enter through the doors into the corridor…"

"And what did you see?"

"The ship was silent."

"Silent?"

"There was absolutely zero activity. No crew. No medical personnel monitoring our status. I floated through the corridors and saw no one. The ship didn't appear in distress. But I did see gigantic asteroids."

"Interesting…go on."

"But what is really mysterious…is I believe I saw Gensys 1 before we even were in its pull."

Jeremiah's face lit up. His mouth dropped open. "You are amazing! You saw all this?"

She looked up at him and nodded slowly.

"Oh that is fascinating," he said. "And you are definitely special!"

Vega One was crippled but functional.

With navigation systems offline, the bridge crew trained their eyes manually – looking for curvature and the seepage of color. Counselor Abagail walked over towards the expansive windows and looked outwards. There was a certain feeling of peace and serenity that overtook her. The stars out in this interstellar galaxy were somehow different than what she had seen before. And even in her childhood, back on Earth, while looking upwards in the sky, through her telescope, she would always admire the stars.

"Look daddy!" she cried. "Look at that beautiful star! It's so bright!"

Daddy approached her and leaned inwards to the viewfinder. He closed his one eye and studied for a few moments. Little Abby stood next to Daddy, her eyes bright and filled with wonder, a big smile plastered across her face.

"Hmm…no," he said.

Her face fell.

"That's not a star," he said. "You found Venus! You found a planet, Abby!"

She squealed. "Let me see! Let me see!"

She looked back through the telescope, a round star scape in the viewfinder, surrounded by black. "It's so bright and pretty!"

Counselor Abagail wiped a tear from her cheek as she pressed her face against the clear glass hull. "The stars are so different yet still the same."

As she studied the vast sea of tiny, white spheres, she listened to Jeremiah speak with Copernicus behind her.

"I believe Abby will find it," he said.

Copernicus raised his eyes and looked at Jeremiah.

"She has a trained eye," Jeremiah added.

"Hmm," Copernicus said, as they all studied the star scape. "The science of it all is interesting. What we did back there – with Gensys 1 – should be impossible."

Counselor Abagail turned around. "Having some faith can make the impossible possible." She returned to gazing out the windows.

Jeremiah looked at Copernicus and raised his eyebrows. He shrugged his shoulders. "There's a lot here that can't be explained," he said. Copernicus continued looking ahead, but nodded as Jeremiah spoke.

"Like…how did we not detect a worm hole right at the entry to the Jovian system? Or even more so…what happened to the crew when we were in stasis?"

Copernicus turned and looked at Jeremiah. "You think there is another force at work here?"

Jeremiah shrugged again.

"I don't know. I can't be certain about anything. But the cosmos are so incredibly mysterious – so unexplored – how can we know *what* to expect?"

Copernicus nodded. "True. The universe is so vast, even we Vegans travel mainly between Vega and the Milky Way. There are so many galaxies. Infinite."

Jeremiah stretched his arm out towards the windows. "But here…we don't know where we are. We're in uncharted territory. And Gensys 1 is clearly in a movement pattern. I remember when the Space Administration was so excited when they found her."

"It's interesting how we happened to encounter her."

Jeremiah nodded. "She was beautiful."

"And deadly."

He nodded again. "We defied science. Sometimes we have to do that."

Copernicus looked at him and cracked a smile. "You are one smart man, Jeremiah. Interesting perspective." And then he leaned in close and lowered his voice. "I want to make sure you go get evaluated before you head to the surface of

Europa. I want to make sure you are functioning properly."

Jeremiah nodded. "Understood."

Counselor Abagail squinted her eyes, looking out towards the dark star palette. There had to be an indicator of where the worm hole could be. She remembered studying them in college astronomy.

"Look for the curvature," her professor had said. "You can see them, but they can close. Or they can move."

She was brought back to the present. Had that really been so many years ago? Had they really been drifting through an uncharted galaxy for nearly fifty years?

And then she thought of the same astronomy class.

"Spacetime is the fabric of the universe," he had explained. "As you travel outwards, away from the Earth, you will be, in essence, traveling backwards in time. Think of all the first radio broadcasts during the dawn of the Industrial age. If you were to be standing on a planet, deep in interstellar space, you would just be picking some of those radio signals up."

She raised her hand and the professor acknowledged her.

"What about time passage in the vicinity of a black hole?"

The professor nodded and raised his eyebrows. "Very good question Miss Abagail."

"Time will pass more slowly in the vicinity of a black hole. So if you were to be standing on a planet next to a black hole, you would experience two things: there would be a much higher gravity. Quite noticeable. And two, the time would pass normally to *you* on the intergalactic planet, but back on Earth – "

"– Time would pass much more quickly. Yes Miss Abagail. So, in essence, a black hole slows the passage of time."

On the ship, so many years later, she squinted, looking for the curvature in space time. Where the stars would look tilted off their axis. Where the cosmic dust would filter out in pastel color, not just floating but directing.

She gasped and turned around. Copernicus looked up from the command console.

"Forty seven Earth years, right?" she asked. "That's how long we've been drifting?"

He nodded.

"Can you run the ship data backwards?"

"Yes, we can."

She joined Copernicus at the console as data filled the screen. "I remembered a lecture I attended in college," she said. "And we had specifically discussed black holes and their effect on space time."

He nodded. "Go on."

"So time is passing much more slowly in this galaxy, right?"

He looked over at her and nodded again. "Yes. Much more so. The extreme gravity and the time passage go hand in hand."

"So we haven't *actually* been drifting for forty seven years, have we?"

"Not in this galaxy. Based on data, I put us at a very recent arrival. That's why I'm quite confident we will find the worm hole. There's only a slim chance that it would have moved or closed in that short amount of time."

She clapped her hands and squealed. "Yes! I know we will find it!"

He smiled. "You're ready, Counselor Abagail. Now do you see why you have been chosen to lead the Ice Moon mission?"

She paused and looked at Copernicus in the eyes. His eyes were tender. He was like the warm, loving father that she missed so. She reached and gave him a hug. "Thanks for helping me see that." And then she leaned back and stood. "Now let me get back to the observation station."

He shook his head. "No need to. Look out there."

She turned and gasped.

It was so beautiful.

So cosmic.

It was like the palette of stars bent inwards, revealing a tunnel, as if someone took a gigantic mirror and everything were reflecting back in on itself.

She thought it looked like a painting.

As if she were standing in a gallery of art; with the colors of a bountiful pallet and a cascade of color reaching inwards towards darkness. The bending brushed the brilliant gases inwards; the stars were surrounding.

"It's so beautiful…" she said, her mouth hanging open, as she shook her head slowly back and forth.

Copernicus sounded the alarm as a digitized announcement followed:

PREPARE FOR WORM HOLE ENTRY!

She found a chair at the nearest empty console and pulled the straps over her shoulders and settled herself into the seat. The crew followed suit as each of the stations were secured and the crew members strapped in.

Copernicus stood at the command console as the announcement sounded again.

PREPARE FOR WORM HOLE ENTRY!

In medical, Moses and Winston strapped Eli onto the raised bed he was resting on, while the medical staff locked all of the cabinets. Winston tapped Moses on the shoulder. "What can we expect going through this? You've been through many of these before, right?"

Moses nodded.

He finished securing Eli, who was in sedation. "He'll sleep through it, thank God. Eli always seems to get so upset during these things."

Back on the bridge, Counselor Abagail sat in her crewman's chair holding tight onto the armrests as the ship got closer and closer to the swirling pastel colors. She turned around and saw Copernicus sitting at the command console. "Hang tight," he said. "The ride could get bumpy."

She grasped the chair as the ship jolted. "Woah!" she said.

"It could get worse," Copernicus said.

On the bridge, they stood watching through the vast windows.

Counselor Abagail watched as the star scape bent inwards, as if they were entering a vast tunnel, where the stars bordered and rounded the threshold, reflecting inwards.

And then the ship rumbled as the worm hole sucked them into its velocity; light flashed past like bright cosmic windows, again, repeatedly.

There was a bright blue flash.

Copernicus stood and held onto the command console. "Man stations!"

Counselor Abagail watched the cosmic masterpiece, her head cocked to the side. She ignored the turbulence. As the ship rocked and jolted, she was not fazed. The lights flashed by as her eyes glassed over.

And there she saw her father.

Like they were streaming through a vast telescope, towards the cosmic viewfinder filled with dust and stars. She saw his arms wrap around her, his smile and his teeth; she could feel his strong arms.

She could touch him.

Smell him.

Feel his embrace.

And then she saw the blue.

The tint.

The colorful gases.

And she started to mutter. "I see the ice…I see the ice…I see the ice…I see it!" She broke her trance and looked back at the bridge, her eyes wide, her mouth open in laughter, tears streaming down her cheeks.

"The Ice Moon! Oh good *God* she's so glorious!"

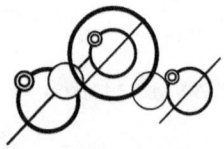

The Ice Moon.

THE POWDER BLUE TINTED LAYER of thick, deep ice, across the vast sphere, in the shadows of the soaring pastel gas cloud networks of Jupiter, in the cosmic thrust of her gravitational pull, there was the orbit of the ice moon of Europa.

Her network of orange veins, thought to be cracks in the ice, looked like hastily assembled puzzle pieces; a patchwork of veins on a powder blue icy skin. She was the perfect sphere; Jupiter was a gargantuan brilliance of color behind her, and she looked tiny in the forefront, but beyond, the tiny, white stars reached outwards for millennia, for light-years, beyond the distant, through the interstellar.

But there was a feeling of contentment and awe from them as they stood on the observation deck.

The vast windows were like a soaring mural of color; *The Jovian System* it would have been called, had it been art hanging in a gallery in the Earthly cities in the past.

Counselor Abagail released her safety harness and stood. She turned around and saw Copernicus was standing, looking down, studying the control panels on the command station.

"I'm heading to medical! This is amazing! I have to see the others!"

The doors slid open and she ran down the corridor towards medical as fast as she could. She ran past several crew members who pressed for her to slow down, but she ignored them. Once at medical, the doors slid open and she burst inside. Eli was sitting up on one of the examination tables, and Winston was seated in a chair nearby. They both looked up at her.

"You guys have to come see it! The worm hole was still right in the same spot. We're on approach of the Jovian system. It's so beautiful!"

Eli's face lit up and he smiled. He looked over at the medical attendant. The attendant nodded and Eli tossed the blanket aside and eased himself onto the floor.

Counselor Abagail looked at Winston and then back at Eli "How's your head?"

Eli pulled on a pair of his regulation pants. "Just a mild concussion. But I'm feeling much better now."

He was excited and back to his old self. The three headed out and down the corridor. As they approached the bridge, Eli walked over to the side and peered out.

"I can see so much from here!" Eli pressed his face against the thick, clear material as his breath steamed it up. He reached up and wiped the mist away.

The doors to the bridge slid open with a hiss and Jeremiah walked through. He carried himself with confidence; walking tall and determined.

Jeremiah joined Eli and placed his arm around his shoulder as Winston and Counselor Abagail stood looking out at the colors of Jupiter.. He pointed at the tiny sphere in front of the gas giant; pointing towards the small, dark, round silhouette in the foreground. "That's Europa," he said. "That tiny little circular thing is the ice moon they were talking about. But it won't be tiny when we get there."

Eli gasped and shook his head. "It looks like a black dot on an ocean of swirling color…"

"Because it is."

They both turned around to see who the voice was. Moses joined them. He smiled wanly, his arms clasped behind his back as he approached the team. Counselor Abagail was tying her red hair behind her head in a neat pony-tail, and turned to face Moses. Eli was still admiring the celestial show before them.

"How much longer until we approach orbit?" Jeremiah asked, looking at Counselor Abagail, and then over at Moses.

"We are farther away than you might think," he said.

"How far?" Jeremiah asked.

"I just came from a briefing, and they told me another few weeks until we are in orbit."

Jeremiah scoffed. "How is that even possible?"

As Jeremiah stood, watching through the expansive windows, Counselor Abagail gently placed her hand on his shoulder. She leaned close to his ear. "Everything is so vast," she said. "We can see so far...but to travel there...we are limited to the physical."

Jeremiah turned to look at her. He placed his arm around her and smiled, as they both looked out at the cosmic magnificence of Jupiter.

"Isn't she beautiful?" Counselor Abagail asked.

He nodded. "It's like nothing I have ever seen before.

She admired the swirling gas giant planet. The layers of bright, pastel colors, swirling around the sphere in different rotating directions. She had previously only seen photos of Jupiter in textbooks and computer images.

"You've seen the star, haven't you?"

Jeremiah squeezed her lightly. She looked up at him, her eyes wide. "The wandering star? Is that what you called it back on Earth?"

He let out a soft chuckle.

"I had many encounters with that star," he said. "At first it seemed like a dream to me."

She nodded.

"And after a while, I started to believe that I was hallucinating."

"But you weren't, were you?"

He looked down and shook his head. "No, I wasn't."

Counselor Abagail took a breath, held it for a moment, and exhaled. "So," she said. "I think I saw Gensys 1 long before we encountered it."

"Yes, I remember you telling us. It made me think."

She started to speak but he cut her off. "Gensys 1 is not the wandering star," he said. "That was a black hole. That's not what the wandering star is."

She looked into his eyes. "Which star is then?"

He shrugged. "It's a mystery, Abby." He returned his gaze to Jupiter. "All of this, it's just one big, gigantic mystery. The cosmos is the biggest, greatest mystery of the scientific world. There's so much of it that's unexplored."

"Do you think we will ever make it to Vega?"

He looked back at her, smiled and nodded. "One of the things the wandering star taught me – the most significant lesson that I took from my interactions with the star – was that science cannot exist without faith. And faith cannot exist without science."

She raised her eyebrows. "Interesting."

He nodded. "I understand the science of our predicament. But I have faith that we will make it to Vega. That our kind will live on."

She looked down, closed her eyes and shook her head. "But the survivors. All lost."

He reached out and lifted her chin. She raised her eyes to him. "But we have the DNA we were looking for from The Red Outpost back on Mars, remember? Our mission there was a success!"

She smiled softly.

"Now it's your turn," he said. "You are our leader on Europa. I will not challenge you. And Eli and Winston support you as well."

She nodded. "I have a nervous feeling in my stomach. I can feel it. Each time I look out at the small moon in the foreground – I am equally awed but so anxious."

"You're a scientist," he said. "You have the technical knowledge to lead a successful mission. This mission to Europa is equally exciting as it is anxiety inducing. Yes, we don't really know what to expect. We've never been to that surface. We just have the data from probes and studies. If Copernicus says there is a portal underneath that icy surface, then we should explore that."

She studied the small sphere in front of swirling Jupiter. Could there really be a portal? And where would it lead?

"All we can do is look. And find out if it's really there. But now it's time to take a leap of faith."

She sighed, and took a few steps closer to the windows. When she was a little girl, she loved to use her telescope at night, and to view the stars and planets. It had been her childhood dream to walk the cosmos as an astronaut. And this mission – what had initially been a rescue mission from a dying planet – has turned to an exploration mission.

Could the portal on Europa – if it actually were to exist – lead to a habitable world? Could they enter and find a new life, populate a new Earth in a different galaxy with human DNA?

She turned and looked at Jeremiah, who had joined Winston and Eli and their admiration of the Jovian system. It seemed so unlike Jeremiah to acquiesce and give her total control. She remembered, back on Earth in Sector B, how often he challenged Elder Cane for power over the colony. But here? In the cosmos? He was giving her total power and cooperation?

She sighed and looked back at the Ice Moon.

And thought of Mars.

So many millions of miles away. So much closer to the planet she had once called home. She thought of those on Earth who had chosen to stay behind. And wondered how much time they would have left with dwindling rations.

But as her mind registered what she was looking at – the tiny sphere against the gaseous pastel palette – she couldn't get the images of

Mars out of her mind. And of the three mounds of dirt.

Could they have been graves?

And whose graves were they?

The doors to the bridge opened with a hiss and everyone turned and saw Copernicus approaching them. "We are through the worm hole," he said. "The crew can handle it now." He approached Moses and leaned close to him, whispering in his ear. Copernicus then turned and headed down the corridor, his back to the group. After a moment, Moses clasped his hands together. "Well, everyone," he said. "We still have some time before we launch you to Europa, so I urge you all to return to your quarters. Eat and rest."

Counselor Abagail raised her eyebrows when she saw Inikia approach Moses and stand next to him.

Moses continued. "I know Counselor Abagail is quite familiar with Inikia. But the rest of you…do you remember her?"

They nodded. "I remember her showing us the solarium of the Vegan plant life," Winston said, giving her a nod.

"Wonderful," Moses said. "She will guide you to your new quarters. You'll be staying in the Vegan sector of the ship from now on." He glanced over at Inikia and nodded. He slowly turned and left, giving the team a nod.

Eli wandered to the other side of the corridor and sat back and leaned against the cool steel wall opposite of the viewing area. He closed his eyes and sighed. "It's so different out here," he said. "So vast. Nothing like Earth at all."

She shifted her face. "What do you mean?"

He opened his eyes just a bit, glancing over at her. She was opening a water canister. "Well the breathing apparatus," he said. "I just can't get used to it. And we're supposed to drill through the ice? On Europa?" He looked around at the others who were resting in a nearby relaxation room.

Winston leaned back in a recliner and was reading a book.

"Hey!" Eli said.

Winston looked up and raised his eyebrows.

Eli looked over at Winston and gave him a big, strong hug. "Let's relax. And get ready."

As they waited and rested in their new quarters in the weeks on the approach to the Jovian system, they spent much of their waking hours together. They did not have the same issues as previous – no longer did they have to drain the fluid from their knees.

And when they would awaken, they did not experience the amnesia they had previously.

During breakfast on the day of the mission, Winston looked over at Eli and shook his head but said nothing, looking downwards as Eli was slowly turning the page of the paperback he was reading.

Winston leaned forward resting his elbows on his knees. "What book is that?"

Eli raised his eyes and looked over at Winston. "It's a book called *The Ice Moon*."

Jeremiah took a sip of coffee and leaned over and peered at Eli's book. "You are reading a book about space exploration?"

He took the book and held it against his chest. "It's about Europa. I found it in the ship library."

Counselor Abagail raised her eyebrows and looked directly at Eli, still holding her mug. "I thought the library was destroyed with Town Square?"

Eli shook his head. "That one was. But I found another one the other day. In this area. I think it's the Vegan library?"

Counselor Abagail's mouth dropped open. "You mean…extra-terrestrial books? How would they even be in English?"

"This one I remember from Earth. There were quite a few books that were familiar."

Jeremiah picked up the book and held it in front of his face. "How interesting," he said. "How they have taken such an interest in our culture…and still such an archaic format given their technological advancement."

They heard footsteps approach their table. They looked up as Moses and Copernicus stood together.

"We have studied your kind for many generations," Copernicus said. "And we have taken painstaking efforts to preserve your way of life over that time period."

"But I think you will find that our ways are far more similar to yours than you may believe," Moses said.

"Anyway," Copernicus said. "Please report to the Launch Chamber."

Winston nodded, placed a bookmark in his page, and closed the book. He leaned back, as his eyes looked downwards at Eli. He breathed in through his nose and continued looking over at Eli. "Do you honestly think the answers are in this book?"

Eli shrugged his shoulders. "Well there must be something! Some chronicle of the past missions?"

Winston shook his head. "No, Eli. That's all merely speculation. This is the first mission to Europa."

After they were prepped and suited, they stood in the outer chamber as the sun shield lifted, revealing the small, icy blue sphere; a planet which they had only studied up until that point.

As they looked at one another and experienced the same things, the same cosmic visions, piece by piece, the tapestries of their minds were gradually sewn together.

When Counselor Abagail looked over towards Jeremiah, she could remember him.

While her memories of Sector B did not flood her mind and leave her awash with reflection, his smile, closely cropped hair, the way he carried himself and pressed himself against the glass admiring Europa and Jupiter with the others, reminded her of who he once was while they spent their years together in Sector B.

He looked over at her and they made eye contact. He cracked a smile.

Their minds met.

Connected.

A certain unseen electricity was in the air, flowing between each of their minds as they stood, watching in silence as the ship hovered towards the vastness of swirling Jupiter.

It was if they could reach out and touch her spinning clouds of gases; the planet which man had studied for many years; but never was able to explore directly until now.

"Four seven, descent initiating."

Counselor Abagail watched the doors close together. And she felt the thud as their pod separated from Vega One. She turned her head to the right, and saw Eli make the Sign of the Cross. Winston's eyes were closed, and Jeremiah turned and made eye contact with her. "This is it," he said. "No other humans have done what we are about to do."

She sighed.

It was much easier to communicate in these suits. She could speak normally, hear the others normally, and that felt better than Mars. The human technology seemed so primitive and constricting. Full of air, and hard to move around.

These alien suits…were like wearing clothes that breathed.

But her impression of the atmospheric suits was dwarfed when she turned and looked through the clear slits across from where they were sitting.

She gasped. "It's – "

She heard Jeremiah chime in on the audio. "Jupiter…" he said. "And we're about to get close to her…"

She saw the pastel through the sliver.

"Radiation shield engaged."

Jeremiah took the helm as she watched the giant rotating pastel sphere of Jupiter in the foreground.

2

THE
COSMIC
POPULACE

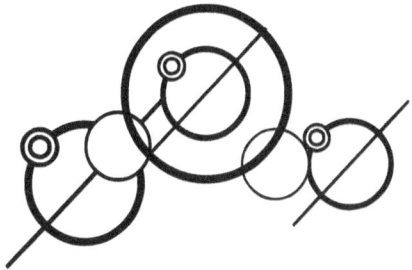

THE POD TOUCHED DOWN with a thud.

They looked out the front windows and remained speechless. The field of ice before them was a hint of powder blue, reflecting the pinks and oranges of the gigantic Jupiter which filled the sky. The ice moon was filled with a darkness that never saw the light of day, but the reflections from the colors of Jupiter offered the cosmic masterpiece they each hold only dreamed of until this day.

Eli opened the back port door as the audio alarm indicated the loss of atmosphere.

315

"Wait!" Counselor Abagail said. "We are going to do this together. Man has never set foot on the icy surface of Europa in all of recorded history. This is going to be a group effort."

Winston and Eli stood by the outer door as Jeremiah headed from the cockpit. Jeremiah reached forward and disengaged the door. It let out a lengthy hiss. He turned around and nodded. Counselor Abagail saw the reflection of his teeth through his helmet visor. He gave a thumbs up and swung the door outwards.

She stepped on the ice.

It was hard and dry.

The terrain was flat and when she looked to her right, there was a field of stars. Further out Vega One waited in orbit. To her left, Jupiter filled the sky with its swirling layers of pastel gases, rotating throughout the sphere. Winston appeared behind her with a radiometer.

"The radiation is intense from Jupiter," he said. "It's off the scale."

She turned and looked at Winston whose face was peering downwards, studying the instrument. "Have some confidence in the Vegans!" she said. "These suits were designed specifically for this mission."

Winston looked up and nodded. "My only concern, with these radiation levels, is how life would survive these conditions? We don't know until we excavate, and even then, what will happen to the environment once we break through this icy shell?"

Jeremiah had been walking the area immediately surrounding the ship. He joined Counselor Abagail and Winston. "We don't know," Jeremiah said. "But if Copernicus is right – if there is a portal under the ice on this moon – then, historically, we need to find it."

Winston handed the radiometer to Jeremiah. Counselor Abagail leaned in close to see it as well. She raised her head and looked over at Winston as Jeremiah started punching in the reset code.

"We expected this, Winston," she said. "Now is not the time to bring up radiation concerns." She looked up towards the open pod outer door. "Eli! What did you find?"

Eli appeared through the ship door. She could see the whites of his eyes through the visor.

"What is it, Eli?"

He climbed down to the surface and joined the others. Counselor Abagail watched him approach, and despite the visor and the darkness, his face was painted with defeat.

"We landed in the wrong spot," he said. "The drill is 22 kilometers *that* way." He pointed straight ahead.

Everyone turned to look. The terrain was flat and icy up to the point of the horizon. At the very edge, where the icy ground met the cosmic sky, there were the shadows of a ridge.

Winston's voice came through the helmet audio. "That's a surface crack," he said. "So the drill is probably on the other side."

"We have to plan how to get across the crack," Counselor Abagail said.

"There's a hook and rope gun in the pod," Eli offered.

Counselor Abagail shook her head. "No, the surface cracks can be seen from orbit. So they have to be miles wide. At the very least."

She looked over at Jeremiah, "We're going to have to climb down and climb back up."

She turned to face Jeremiah, who was looking outwards towards the horizon. He turned around and faced the others. "What about bringing the drill to us? Can we do that somehow?"

"We just have the same problem in reverse," Winston said.

"Can't we just move the pod?" Eli asked.

"We don't have the power reserves," Winston said. "It doesn't work that way. MACA 1 is designed to land on the surface and launch back to Vega One. It's not a surface transport vehicle."

"And we don't have a ROVER," Jeremiah added. "Not that it would matter once we approached the ridge."

Counselor Abagail turned back around and faced the horizon. "We could walk," she said. "It might take some time, but the surface cracks are jagged. There might be a point in the distance where we could walk around the crack and approach the drill."

"I'm going to contact Vega One," Jeremiah said, heading back to the pod.

"Let's all go back to the pod and take a break from these helmets and think this through," she said. "We don't have time to waste."

They nodded and followed.

Once they were back up inside the pod, Winston closed the door with a lengthy hiss. The monitor in the captain's chair livened.

ATMOSPHERIC PRESSURE
STABILIZING

They sat in four chairs facing each other in their suits and helmets until an audio tone sounded from above.

PRESSURE STABILIZATON COMPLETE

They removed their helmets.

Jeremiah raised his eyes. "Computer. Contact Vega One."

They swiveled their chairs around to face a flat wall monitor. Counselor Abagail looked over at Jeremiah and leaned forward. She made eye contact with him and nodded. He nodded in return.

After a few moments, Copernicus and Moses appeared on the screen. They were sitting in the bridge but the crew was not surrounding them in the stations. Copernicus looked concerned.

"Where's the crew?" Counselor Abagail asked.

Copernicus shook his head. "They are assisting engineering. We've sustained some damage from the wormhole. We've lost a significant amount of power and Jupiter's gravitational pull is slowly pulling us towards her."

Her mouth dropped open and she looked over at the others.

Jeremiah shrugged his shoulders as Winston leaned back in his chair and folded his arms. Counselor Abagail returned to the monitor. "So you're in a holding pattern right now?"

Copernicus shook his head but Moses replied. "We're in a state of emergency right now. We're drifting towards Jupiter at a slow rate but unable to pull out of it right now."

"What about the thrusters?" Jeremiah asked.

"Negative," Moses said. "They were damaged by Genesys 1 when we were pulling from the gravity of the black hole. I knew that we would damage them by doing it, but if we hadn't escaped Genesys 1, we would have been vaporized."

Counselor Abagail nodded. "We understand. So you're troubleshooting?"

Moses nodded. "We're attempting to repower but negative success thus far. Now what is your situation down there?"

Counselor Abagail turned and made eye contact with Jeremiah, then Winston, and finally Eli. She turned back to the screen and sighed. "We've landed in the wrong location."

Copernicus returned to the screen. "What do you mean you landed in the wrong location?"

"From our instruments down here, the cryobots are 22 kilometers away from us."

Copernicus nodded. "The excessive radiation from Jupiter is affecting your navigation. We haven't the technology yet to combat that."

"What about the cryobots?" Jeremiah asked. "Are they in the right landing location?"

"They have a homing beacon," Copernicus said.

Counselor Abagail leaned closer towards the screen. "We were planning on walking. But there looks to be the shadow of a ridge in the distance. From what we've studied about Europa, that would be a massive crack in the surface, correct?"

Moses nodded. "Yes. Europa's surface is filled with them. And you won't be able to scale the crack." On the screen, they saw Copernicus head towards one of the terminals on the far wall of the bridge. "I'm checking our historical data," he called back. "I can't show anything gathered in live time because of the damage we sustained but I can pull up the saved mapping from before. We've mapped Europa a number of times during pass-bys."

Counselor Abagail nodded and looked at the others for approval.

"It's going to be a long, frigid walk," Winston said quietly. "Average temperature is -220 degrees Celsius."

"And there are ice quakes," Jeremiah added.

Counselor Abagail nodded. "I'm not sure we have much of a choice."

Moses leaned in closer towards the screen as Copernicus remained at the workstation along the far wall. Moses lowered his voice. "Our situation is dire," he said. "Copernicus won't tell you that," he said. "But if we do not get power to Vega One, it will collide with Jupiter."

She gasped and her eyes widened. "You can't orbit?"

"That's a negative," Moses said. "We were unsuccessful in our last attempt and with such reduced power, we are drifting."

"How many are on board?" Jeremiah asked.

"We have three hundred still on board," Moses said. "And plenty of pods in the launch chambers to abandon ship. The pods are only designed for landing and launching back to the mother ship. The only place we could go is down to Europa. And that's why we must find the portal. The cryobots have been recording data since the drilling began, so you just need to locate them."

Counselor Abagail shook her head. "The survivors were lost when the ship was damaged. But we are still here, and you can still be saved," she said, looking over at the others. "But…how do we know where this portal *leads*? If it even will take us where you believe it will go?"

"We don't know," Moses said. "But in these times of uncertainty, one has to learn to trust. A lot will depend on what you find down there. Hopefully that will give us some answers to go on. And then after that, it becomes a leap of faith."

A leap of faith.

Counselor Abagail and Jeremiah made eye contact. Jeremiah nodded as she smoothed the side of her hair. She looked back up at the screen. "Okay," she said. "So this has turned into a rescue mission. We have to find that portal."

Everyone turned to look at Eli. He looked up. "Hopefully there will be some clues as to where it leads."

Copernicus rushed back to the screen. "Ah ha! I have found a break in the ridge where you can pass over. It will be just to the north – on the pole side – of your present location."

Counselor Abagail looked at the team. "We don't have time to waste. Let's get our helmets back on and get out there. We have to find the cryobots and see how much of the ice they've melted through."

"We wish you God's speed," Copernicus said as Moses looked at him. "Gravity there is only thirteen percent of Earth's, so you will find you will move quite differently than you are used to. Be careful of ice quakes which can strike randomly. And water plumes."

Eli looked up. "Water plumes?"

"There is an ocean beneath the icy surface," Copernicus explained. "Water can shoot upwards through the cracks in the ice out into space. Be very careful of these. Due to the low gravity, a plume can force you off the surface."

"We will lose communication while you are out of the pod," Moses said. "So God's speed and good luck."

The team got up and started to put on their helmets. "We can drag AMPHIBIA along with us," Winston said. "She's super light. Like a sled."

Counselor Abagail nodded. "Eli, put the equipment on top of her and get her secure." She turned over to Jeremiah. He stood, his helmet on and ready, and looked directly at her. "We can do this," he said. "All hope is not lost."

She closed her eyes for a moment and nodded. She hoisted her helmet up and they joined the others outside.

Winston and Eli dragged AMPHIBIA out of the equipment compartment and slammed the door. "She'll power up once she submerges," Jeremiah said, standing next to Counselor Abagail. "She runs on liquids."

"Okay," she said, looking at Eli. "You have the rope gun and pickaxes? I don't know how deep this is going to be. I doubt there'll be a set of stairs."

Eli nodded. "All ready and secured."

They started the journey.

Eli dragged AMPHIBIA behind them as Jeremiah fell back to assist him. Counselor Abagail looked over at Jupiter and stopped walking for a moment. "Listen," she said. Winston stopped walking and looked up as Jeremiah and Eli caught up and stopped walking, their boots trudged on the ice.

"Do you hear that?" Counselor Abagail asked.

Jeremiah dropped the rope and stood next to Counselor Abagail.

"It's...like some sort of weird music," she said, watching the rotating pastel gas giant, shaking her head. "Like a long, deep note playing...over and over. Holding and building its own crescendo for infinity."

"Impressive, counselor," Winston said.

"I was first cellist," she said. "Before the shift, of course."

She turned and saw Eli staring at Jupiter. She could see the reflection in the whites of his eyes through his helmet visor. "It's coming from Jupiter," he said. "I remember from my astronomy class. It's the vibration of electromagnetic particles...they create these sounds when they collide...it's like a song. Beautiful and eerie at the same time."

"So we have a soundtrack to our mission!" Jeremiah said. "It's beautiful, but we have to keep moving."

Counselor Abagail nodded and grabbed the tug rope. "Take a break, Eli. I'll drag her for a while."

He nodded and started ahead.

"Lead the way, Eli," Jeremiah said, assisting Counselor Abagail with AMPHIBIA. Eli started ahead as the ground started shaking. He lost his footing and fell to the ground.

"Eli!" Jeremiah called. They all fell on the ice as the shaking increased in intensity.

"It's an ice quake!" Winston called. "Hover down!"

Eli was lying a good fifty yards ahead of the others. The ice quake continued shaking as a crack formed ahead and around him.

"Eli!" Winston called. "Get back by us! The cracks are building all around you!"

"Eli!" Counselor Abagail called as she tried to lift herself up.

The shaking stopped and then water exploded out of the crack below Eli, shooting him from the surface, upwards and outwards. They looked up and saw him in a cloud of water vapor; the escaping plume they had been warned about. Through the crack and up into space.

"Eli!" they called out. They each got to their feet and ran towards the plume of water vapor, but they couldn't get too close. When Counselor Abagail looked up at Eli, he was higher…and higher…caught by the gravitational pull and heading towards Jupiter.

Winston screamed. "Eli!"

Counselor Abagail felt tears well into her eyes. She grabbed Jeremiah's arm. "We have to save him! If he enters Jupiter's orbit he will die!"

"Abby! There is nothing we can *do*! He is too high to retrieve. We have no contact with Vega One! And we are too far from the pod to get the retriever line!"

"Eli!" she called. "Talk to us!"

There was static but he was trying to speak.

"I am fine," he said amidst the heavy static. "No pain…no pain at all…"

"No, Eli!" she said. "You aren't going to die today!" She tore through the equipment and aimed the rope gun up at Eli, who was now drifting in orbit above the ice moon.

"Don't use it," he said through crackling static. "You will need that. Let me drift. I will be fine…no pain…no pain there will be…"

She looked at massive Jupiter swirling behind him.

"No, you won't be *fine*!"

She turned to Jeremiah. He placed his hands on her arms. She looked up at him, and made eye contact through their visors. "We have to save him! The gases will kill him!"

Jeremiah closed his eyes and shook his head. "He won't have any pain, Abby."

"What are you talking about? How could he not have pain?" She looked over at Winston. "Why are you both standing here acting like nothing's wrong?! We just lost a member of our team and no one except me is acting with any type of urgency to save him!"

Jeremiah looked over at Winston and Winston nodded. Jeremiah reached up and unlocked his helmet with a hiss as Counselor Abagail watched in horror.

"No!" she screamed. "Don't! There's too much radiation! You'll die!"

Jeremiah did not listen and removed his helmet. Winston stood in front of her, reached his arm over and placed it on her shoulder.

"Eli will be just fine," Winston said. "He will not have any pain."

She looked up at Winston. He kept his hand on her shoulder and looked at her directly in the eyes. Jeremiah stood and dropped his helmet to the icy surface with a thud. He stood in front of them, standing and watching them. Their eyes met, but he said nothing and remained expressionless.

She gasped.

She had thought there was something different about Jeremiah. Something not quite the same. Ever since they had returned to Vega One from Mars...but still...he was the same. And that caused her to forget about it.

As Jeremiah stood facing her, she looked up and saw that Eli had drifted even further away, closer to the gas giant Jupiter. Jeremiah unclasped his glove and tossed it on the ice. He looked directly at her, never breaking eye contact, as he clasped his wrist and clicked. He held his hand up in front of her face and she gasped.

Several wires and tiny lights blinked in the wrist interior.

Her eyes widened. "You're – you're..."

Winston's helmet clicked and let out a hiss as he dropped his to the ground at his feet. His voice sounded a bit muffled as he was no longer speaking into the helmet auditory system, but she could hear him. "Our DNA was harvested during our first stage of cryogenic hibernation. From Earth to Mars."

"And then we were cloned to robotic androids after Mars," Jeremiah said. "You remember the period on Mars when you woke up and couldn't remember anything?"

She nodded and took a few steps back. "I remember...your space suit, Jeremiah...I remember it lying on its side. Empty."

Winston extended his arms. "You have to trust us, Abby."

She shook her head. "You guys seemed a little different after we got back to Vega One. But I thought it was me..."

Jeremiah took a step forward as Counselor Abagail fell backwards over a small jut of ice. Both he and Winston lunged forward to help her up. She sat on the small, protruding shelf of ice and rested her arms on her legs. She hung her head down for a moment and caught her breath. Winston and Jeremiah both stood a few feet from her, looking down, both appeared concerned.

"Counselor Abagail," Winston said. "Are you alright?"

She looked up at the remaining members of her team. Jeremiah connected his hand back to his wrist connector. "Abby," he said, looking over at her. She looked up at him. "The Vegans have the technology to clone. Not only our genetic codes, but also minute, intricate details of our personalities were imprinted on these physical droid shells. When you were marooned on Mars, we were put in place so the mission would not have upset your life so much, and the ultimate mission – the one we are on now – could continue."

Abby stood. "Can you guys put your helmets back on so I can hear you more clearly? Everything sounds so muffled through mine."

They agreed and reached down and reattached their helmets to their space suits. Now she could hear them loud and clear in her helmet audio system.

She walked over and picked up the tow line. She turned around and gestured for Winston and Jeremiah to follow.

After a few more minutes of walking, she popped the question. "What happened back on Mars, Jeremiah? Why did they have to clone you?"

She instantly thought of the three mounds of dirt. They had to have been graves. "Those three dirt mounds I found near the ridge on Mars…they were graves, right?"

Jeremiah stammered and assisted her with the tow rope as Winston took the lead. "I…don't know…"

"You don't know?"

He looked over at her and nodded. "Yes, I don't know. I have no memory or recollection of what happened on Mars. I was imprinted based on data which was collected before the Mars mission. I have no memories of the time you were on Mars. It just didn't exist for this version of Jeremiah."

"But did they die on Mars? Is that what those dirt mounds were? Did I bury them in graves?"

Jeremiah shrugged his shoulders. "I don't know, Abby. I just don't know. But what we do know – now – is that Eli will not feel any pain when he encounters Jupiter. We don't have pain receptors. We can have a *memory* of pain that occurred before the imprint – but no pain after. We're still the same guys you have always known. New memories are forming in our sub systems as we speak."

"So he's just drifting, lying there, watching the stars?"

He shook his head. "No. When we are in a situation that cannot be remedied and 'death' is inevitable, we are programmed to shut down. Right now, he is just a piece of space junk floating towards a planet that will annihilate him."

"He is *not* space junk!" She looked up. She could see Eli's silhouette, a tiny, dark figure against the swirling pastel palette of Jupiter. He was floating upwards and outwards, and now he was so high, drifting, that he was becoming a tiny dark spot. She could still make out his outstretched arms and legs, and as he drifted closer to annihilation, she felt the warmth of a tear stream down her cheek.

Counselor Abgail listened to the scrape of AMPHIBIA on the ice as she closed her eyes.

Flat terrain from here on out.

Their boots scraped against the ice amidst the lonely cello; the single solitary note against the silence of space playing with a solidarity. She paused and opened her eyes when she heard the footsteps stop. They all looked upwards. Vega One had stopped rotating. She was a lengthy cylinder; and the tube like design had rotated to create synthetic gravity…and an atmosphere.

But not anymore.

She looked over at Jeremiah who was looking upwards, studying the ship. "She's much closer to Jupiter now," he said. "Much, much closer."

"What about the rotation?" Counselor Abagail asked.

"There's no gravity on the ship if it's not rotating," Winston said. "And no atmosphere."

"How will they breathe?" she asked.

"Well," Winston said. "They may have sectioned off a small portion of the ship. Sealed it off. They do have a small amount of emergency power that they can use to create a finite amount of atmosphere and breathable air."

"But it wouldn't last for long," Jeremiah added. "And the ship is drifting closer to Jupiter. The gravitational pull of that planet is forceful. I'm afraid they don't have much time."

They stood at the edge of the ravine.

Counselor Abagail stood on top of a massive cliff; the other side appeared to be at least a mile across. No possible way it could have been scaled. But Copernicus had been right, and they had been heading in the right direction. For they were standing on the edge of the massive crack; there was a way across towards her left. Just a simple walk across.

She scanned the opposite side. There was something ahead, moving, in the distance.

"Are those the cryobots?" she asked. There was a small dark shadow in the distance. Some dark, shadowy, vertical movement. Jeremiah activated his vision enhancement filter and nodded. "Yes, that's them," he said. "I can see the cylinder moving up and down." She activated her own vision enhancement filter on

338

her visor. The pink aura of Jupiter reflected on the ice ahead. She saw the regulation melting cylinder lower itself and disappear into the ice. "That's them," she said. "We're not far." And then she looked up at Vega One. The enhancement zoomed her vision. "I think I saw a pod leave the ship!"

Jeremiah looked up at the ship. "We don't have much time," he said. Counselor Abagail scanned the ship. It was much closer to Jupiter's orbit. "They may be heading to the surface," Winston said. "But are you sure? I don't see any pods."

"Let's go," Counselor Abagail said. They picked up the pace and headed across the massive ravine. She peered over the side as they journeyed across the edge, moving from one side of the crack towards the other; she saw the orange tint – cosmic dust from Jupiter. And outwards, towards the black palette and a field of tiny, white stars.

The sun was out there; the muted light filtered across the ice moon from the extreme distance, giving it a shine. A luster.

And Earth was back there, too.

Earth.

Once it had been her home, all of their homes. Now, many millions of miles away, in a land which felt so foreign, the mission, on a team of two clone droids which somewhat resembled her friends, was more personal; what would home become?

There was a rumble in the ice as they approached the drill site. The cryobots — lengthy cylinders which resembled long, thick poles — were ice melting machines. The pod sat several yards away, and mechanical arms held the cryobot as it disappeared into the ice. The ground shook again. "It's the ice melting," Winston said. "Large chunks must be falling. That means they're further along than I thought." Counselor Abagail and Jeremiah dropped the tow line and peered down into the hole.

It was a deep trench. She could see flashing blue lights on the end of the cryobot as it disappeared into the darkness below. The blue reflected on the edges of the ice as it disappeared from site. She turned around and saw the line connected on the edge of the pod. She turned to Jeremiah who was moving supplies from AMPHIBIA and spreading them out on the surface ice.

"How deep is the ice?" she asked. Jeremiah got up and joined her at the edge.

He peered down, and she looked as well. It was complete blackness again. "We're going to test it when we lower AMPHIBIA. I'd be willing to bet a mile or two at this location. Saved research data from Vega One put this location where the ice thins out – at least somewhat."

Winston was examining the pod connections and called out to the others. "She's hit bottom. I have a visual! There *is* water below! She's stationary on an ice ledge in a cavern of some sort. Heater's off."

They rushed to Winston's side who had opened a panel on the edge of the pod revealing video and audio contact. Counselor Abagail moved close and saw the screen. "The cam ROVER has detached?"

Winston nodded as Jeremiah moved closer as well.

The cryobot was resting in a soaring cavern tinted with the blue lights from the side of the ice melting cylinder. The soaring ceiling reached up and over – but what made Counselor Abagail gasp was the lap of the water – which reached the edge of the ice, lapping, flowing across its edge, and flowing deeper into the darkness.

She shook her head, her eyes wide, studying the picture. "It's…a beach of ice…"

"And the cavern is *huge*!" Jeremiah said.

Winston nodded. "One point two miles, straight down."

"How do we know the portal is down there?" Jeremiah asked.

Counselor Abagail watched as monitors confirmed the chemical composition of the water. "We don't," she said. "But if this cavern is there, there might be more. And the signal – Copernicus said it was originating from this area."

Winston laughed and clapped his hands. "Unbelievable!"

They both looked at his data. "It's seawater!" he exclaimed. Through his visor, he beamed with a smile. "This is unbelievable! I had studied this planet for years. There were always rumors of an under ice ocean. And then Maximillian confirmed it, but that was just before the shift back on Earth. So the data just sat there. And the research stopped. But now…"

"Maximillian?" she asked.

"You don't remember them?" Winston asked. "They were huge in astrobiology before the shift. Then they went under with the rest of the world."

She nodded. "Ah, yes. I remember now. Those pressure bubbles were their project. Could have used those here. Now it's time to go down there and complete our mission," Counselor Abagail said.

"Well the Vegan technology is far more advanced," Winston said. "And AMPHIBIA is brilliant."

Jeremiah didn't waste any time and hoisted AMPHIBIA up and carried it towards the shaft. "She'll power up once she hits the water. But we'll have to go down and give her the final push, or she'll just sit on the edge of the ice like an idiot. We don't want to risk going any deeper. She'll train on the beacon once she powers up."

Counselor Abagail nodded as Winston closed the panel on the edge of the pod when the ground shook violently, knocking each of them off their feet. There was a bright orange reflection on the surface ice as Counselor Abagail looked up, and screamed.

"Abby! Winston!" Jeremiah called. "Are you okay?!"

Their vision was clouded with a black vapor.

The ground continued to shake as she turned on her stomach. She struggled to lift herself up on the shaking, slippery ice, and turned her head towards the sky.

A series of bright flashes emanated from the sky closer towards Jupiter.

"Where is the ship!? *Where is Vega One?!*"

She felt Jeremiah's strong arm grab hers as the blackness cleared. "Winston! Winston come in!"

She looked up towards Jupiter. It was confirmed.

Vega One was gone.

She screamed. "No!"

She instantly thought of Copernicus. And Inikia. And Moses. She propped herself up on her elbows and hung her head down until the edge of her helmet tapped the ice. Had they escaped? And what about the others?

"Winston!" Jeremiah said. "Winston come in!" The shaking subsided and Jeremiah rose to his feet. He ran towards the pod. Counselor Abagail turned around as Jeremiah retreated around the far end of the pod. "Don't come back here, Abby!"

She hoisted herself up. "What is it Jeremiah?"

"*Don't come back here Abby! Just wait there!*"

She shuffled her feet along the ice and kept her focus on Jeremiah. He was on his knees. She could make out Winston's boots. Was he injured? But how could he be injured if he was a clone droid?

As she rounded the corner, she gasped.

Jeremiah was kneeling, his head hung low. And Winston was lying, flat on his back, with a massive piece of metal which had split his abdomen. She shook her head and ran towards Winston and fell to her knees. Jeremiah grabbed her arms and started to pull her away. She fought and pried his hands off her arm.

"I told you to stay put!" he said.

She shook her head. "No!"

There had been no blood, only the severing of wires and cables. The metal cut a jagged edge just above the waist.

"We can't just leave him here," she said, looking down and shaking her head. Jeremiah got up and started punching the code for the pod interior access panel. "We can put him inside. We have no means to bury him."

She sighed and scanned the surface area. The orbit near Jupiter had calmed and the surface ice once against reflected the pink and orange pastels of the gas giant. "I don't see any signs of their pod anywhere," she said.

"Well there are three things that could have happened," Jeremiah said as the door slid open with a hiss. He climbed inside the darkness and started checking panels for power. "One. They didn't make it off Vega One and were vaporized in the explosion."

"Let's try to think more positively," she said, getting to her feet and looking down at Winston. The metal that sliced him in half was at least twice her height and at least several feet across. She looked up towards the sharp peak of metal. A cosmic cloud levitated above.

"Two," he said. "They managed to escape in a pod but didn't clear the explosion and were vaporized in the blast."

"Jeremiah…"

"I'm just being a realist," he said. "And three. They made it to the surface, and the force of the explosion could have knocked them severely off track, and they could be on the other side of the moon. Or even on another moon altogether. Jupiter has twenty one moons. I'm working on leaving them a message in case they made it."

She bent down and dragged Winston's legs around the side of the pod. Several multicolored wires hung haphazardly with shredded tubing. As she approached the exterior entry panel, she looked up and saw Jeremiah sitting at the command console. His helmet was off, sitting on the floor beside him. He was typing. He paused, looked over and her, and stepped out onto the ice. He bent over and picked up Winston's leg apparatus. "There is a sleeping area in the back," he said. "We will lay him out on one of the beds and cover him up."

"So what do you feel? Do you think they made it? Or not?"

Jeremiah hoisted Winston's legs into the pod and turned back towards the sleeping chamber. Counselor Abagail saw him shaking his head as he ventured further towards the rear of the pod. "I don't know Abby," he called. "I'm imprinted with Jeremiah's thoughts and feelings, but she hardly heard him through her helmet. His voice was faint and muffled again. She climbed inside and followed him. "I can hardly hear you!"

He gingerly laid the legs at the foot of the bed. He looked up and made eye contact with her, "Don't worry," he called out. "I will put my helmet back on soon so you can hear me better."

He went to the command console and grabbed his helmet, snapping it back into place. She could hear him much more clearly now. "If they made it, then it's quite possible they could locate the cryobots with the power of their escape pod. We don't know if the pod is fully operational. And if they truly *are* on the other side of the moon, it could take weeks to get here. Even longer without any mapping capabilities."

She nodded and jumped outside. She walked around to the other side of the pod to pick up Winston's upper body and head as Jeremiah remained inside and started typing a message for the others.

"Do you think they can survive that long out here?"

"I don't know, Abby. We are merely speculating."

"Try contacting the other pod. Can you?"

She pried Winston from the massive metal sheet. The other half of the multicolored wires and severed tubing dragged along the ice as she pulled Winston towards the pod, her hands wrapped around his forearms, dragging him from behind. She stopped when she reached the outer door. She peered inside and saw that Jeremiah had powered on the command console. Bright, colorful lights traveled across the darkness of the dash. He hovered over the controls and was pecking at a small keyboard.

"Hey, can you give me a hand here?"

Jeremiah looked over at Abby and jumped up. He leaned over the side ladder as Counselor Abagail lifted Winston's arms. Jeremiah grabbed Winston's forearms and lifted his upper body into the pod. He carried it back and placed it on the bed with the other half as Counselor Abagail sat at the command console.

The digital screen mapping the area was empty. Jeremiah returned and took the seat next to her. "Nothing on the command controls. According to MACA 2, the only thing out there is MACA 1 – which is our pod – approximately 22 kilometers *that* way." Jeremiah pointed across the ravine.

"Let's try anyway," she said.

Jeremiah shrugged his shoulders and pressed the communication command button. "This is MACA 2. Does anyone read me? MACA 2 over."

Dead silence.

She looked up at the sky. A clouds of cosmic dust still hovered close to Jupiter – the remnants of Vega One, no doubt, but where had the pieces of metal, the massive, cylindrical hull gone?

Jeremiah finished typing the message. He read it to Counselor Abagail:

EUROPA 1 MISSION TEAM REPORTING. LANDED 22 KILOMETERS FROM CRYOBOT MELTING SITE. EN ROUTE TO PORTAL. MAPPED LOCATION VIA VEGA ONE AND TRAVELED ON FOOT. LOST ELI DUE TO WATER PLUME OUTBURST. WENT OFFLINE AND ABSORBED INTO JUPITER'S ORBIT. VEGA ONE EXPLOSION CAUSED METAL TO SEVER AND SHUT DOWN WINSTON. LEFT MACHINE APPARATUS IN MACA 2 REAR. JEREMIAH WALTER AND JANINE ABAGAIL CURRENTLY ON MISSION. FOLLOW TOW LINE TO LOCATE.

She nodded. "I guess that's all we can do."

A searing, high pitched whistle sounded just above them as a giant section of the hull crashed into the ice just yards away from MACA 2. Counselor Abagail gasped as she watched the smoking metal through the

351

viewfinder. The ground shook knocking them both off their feet.

"Another icequake! Come on, let's get down there!" Jeremiah said. "It's the only safe place right now!"

Jeremiah flashed through the controls, shutting down power as Counselor Abagail huddled by the rear entry.

Jagged pieces of the metal hull for Vega One started raining down at ferocious speeds – some still burning, others charred. Some were as small as the communication screens on their suit arms; another which crashed into the nearby ravine was massive and jutting upwards above the threshold of the cliff.

"Come on, Abby, hurry!"

They ran to the cavern opening as Jeremiah dragged AMPHIBIA and tossed her down the hole. He turned and assisted Abby with her silver, shiny picks and he lifted her, turning her around and positioning her on the edge of the wall. She dug them into the edge of the ice.

"Climb down as fast as you can! I'll send your light rods!" She nodded and moved her right hand down, digging the pick back into the ice. She followed with her left hand. There was far less gravity on this planet than she was used to, and as she looked downwards into the darkness, she thought of the mile-plus that she had to navigate down into the cavern. She looked up one more time and Jeremiah gave her a thumbs up. He threw down several blue glowing light sticks and she reached and grabbed one. The blue light reflected against the wall of ice. She looked up and Jeremiah was gone.

"Jeremiah, come in?"

The connected was filled with static. "Thumbs up, Abby. I'm getting the power pa –"

Dead silence.

"Jeremiah, come in!"

She connected to the tow line and automatically started lowering as another ice quake started. She stopped the lowering and held tight to the line as she rocked back and forth against the ice walls.

"Jeremiah do you read me?!"

As the icequake subsided, she started lowering again. She kept looking up towards the opening, as it grew smaller and smaller. And as she made repeated attempts to contact

Jeremiah, the line filled with static, until her visor projected the message right in front of her eyes:

SIGNAL LOST.

The ice chute grew darker and quieter the lower she traveled down the tow line. The only light was her single, solitary blue rod, which she had nestled in the side of her suit arm. She looked up again.

Just darkness.

Sight of the opening had been lost a while back.

The sounds were gone.

No feelings of icequakes, or the screams of metal charging to the surface.

Would Jeremiah follow her?

She touched down into darkness and silence. The blue light rods that Jeremiah had tossed down earlier lay on the ice floor, each giving a pale glow. She saw the cryobot sitting just a few yards away. It oddly looked like it could be a tree trunk in this strange, cosmic cavern.

Water lapped at the ice a mere few yards away. The cavern was soaring; rounded ice walls leading inwards and deeper into the Europa ice.

Had she been destined for this all along?

Was there some sort of cosmic connection? Her destiny...her same self...there was something about the ice caverns. The solitude and the silence, the blue light and the darkness. Something reassuring, something inviting.

Had Jeremiah, this close, never been destined to journey to this point? To see this beauty? This deep secrets of the ice moon?

And what of the cavern?

The mystical, mysterious cavern which had remained hidden for millennia – neither humans nor Vegans knew of the caverns. But somehow, in some way, Copernicus had known of a portal. But the portal was not in this cavern. The water which lapped at the ice – the edge of the ice beach – held no clues when she glanced at it.

She sat on the ice at the edge of the water and closed her eyes. There had been so much. So much sensory overload. So much information in her mind to download and decompress from.

She hung her head down between her knees and saw the images of Mars flood through her memory. She saw the empty suit. That had been Jeremiah's suit. And now, she was sitting in a cosmic ice cavern, millions upon millions of miles away from that space suit, again wondering where Jeremiah had gone.

But where had he really gone?

For he had been lost to her since Mars – and even after, during the days on Vega One – he had seemed somewhat different, yet the same.

But where had he *really* gone?

She shook her head and opened her eyes.

There was a dark patch in the water.

She crawled a few steps back, and reached her arm out for the closest light stick. She slowly rose to her knees, never taking her eyes off the dark patch in the water.

It appeared to be moving, slowly, perhaps hovering.

She caught her breath in her throat. It could not be. It just *could not be*.

She drew the light stick over towards the water. The blue glow reflected back towards her, but its illumination was sufficient.

There was movement!

She leaned closer, just a small bit, sliding closer to the edge of the water on her knees. "Ohhhh…."

She gasped.

The small white orbs…could they be eyes?

The movement at the edges of the dark patch…were they gills?

And then, it moved closer, looking up at her through the liquid, as if…observing her.

There was a *face*!

Her mouth dropped open and she gasped again.

She shook her head as tears streamed down her face. "You…are…*beautiful*!"

She stared at the being.

At the life before her. At the life staring back at her, through the lapping water, as two species encountered one another for the first time.

She started to signal at it, running her fingers up and down. Could there be communication? Would this creature know about the portal?

Was it intelligent?

Her mind was suddenly flooded with questions that she could not answer. She had remembered, as a student back on Earth, how the common assumption of extra-terrestrial life would be some form similar to a two-legged mammal, but had she ever thought of the first encounter be with amphibian extra-terrestrial life! She had not.

She looked over at AMPHIBIA.

It looked primitive and clunky compared to the swirling black cosmic creature in the water next to her. The creature had long protruding tentacles – dozens of them, it appeared, and one of them splashed upwards through the water. She froze, watching the tentacle appear to beckon her forward.

She took a cautious step back towards the hanging tow line.

Trust Abby.

She heard the words ring through her mind. *Believe in yourself and you are capable of anything.*

She stood and stared at the creature.

It did not move.

It did not attempt to retreat, or attack in any way.

She went to the water's edge once again, and made eye contact with the creature. Its outer fins were swirling like blowing curtains in the wind, as it hovered, waiting patiently.

It cocked its head to the side.

What are you waiting for?

Why are you so afraid?

She fell to her knees.

Jeremiah was gone.

He had to be. There was no more contact. Only a crackling on the communicator.

But there was no ship to go to anyway.

What other choice did she have?

Take a leap of faith…

She stood, feeling her heart beat in her chest. She concentrated on each breath…in…and out…as she brought her left foot forward, close to the water's edge.

As her boots were covered by the laps of the tiny waves, multiple tentacles surfaced, bending in the middle, forming a seat. She stood at the edge of the water watching, her heart beating fast, her eyes open wide, not knowing what to think.

Take the leap of faith...

The sea creature moved closer, as close as it could be while still under the water. Tentacles reached up through the water, now closer, beckoning for her to sit.

She took a deep breath.

And she turned back, looking at the cryobot sitting, just feet from her, and AMPHIBIA, lying on the ice, unused, probably never to be used. And the tow line, her last lifeline to what was somewhat familiar.

She turned back to the waiting creature.

Should she go?

Should she take the leap of faith?

And she took another step forward as the water quickly reached up half her suit.

She felt her heart race as the creature moved the tentacle seat closer towards her.

It's time to trust.

She spilled into the seat, as the creature swam gently back, away from the ice shore, and she saw the equipment grow smaller. It held her as it swam just beneath the surface, holding her tight as several of the tentacles wrapped themselves around her. As they approached the far end of the cavern, she looked down, made eye contact with the creature, and it cocked its head to the side once again.

The tentacles tightened somewhat, but still gently, and she was not in pain. She looked back at the shore, it now seemed distant. And she held her stare, for what seemed like just a moment, as all of the tentacles wrapped around her and pulled her under; and they splashed under the water, deep, rapidly, and forcefully.

She felt the pressure of the water as the creature pulled her through the deep underwater caverns.

She saw the flashes of lights outside her visor as water started to fill her suit. Had there been some sort of a breach? Was there a flaw in their mission specific design?

The water filled her legs, and then her arms and torso, and finally into her helmet as she held her breath.

Would this be the end?

Would this be the finality that she may have been destined to experience; to discover the ice moon; its cosmic under-surface ocean; its life.

But then she shot out of the water with an enormous splash, and onto a sandy beach in a cavern covered in rock. Her legs felt heavy, her muscles fatigued, but she managed to crawl to her knees under the weight of the water she had taken on.

She unlocked her helmet and the water splashed out. Any minute now. It was bound to happen at any given moment. But she could no longer hold her breath in the seawater that had penetrated her space suit.

She dropped her helmet to the sand.

And took a deep breath.

And she exhaled.

Air!

Her head fell back as she closed her eyes, feeling the drips from her hair against the sides of her cheeks. She breathed in, and out again. And she heard the water lapping against the sand.

She mustered the strength to turn around and opened her eyes. The creature was still floating underneath the water, its outer gills still looking like fans blowing back and forth.

It levitated and looked directly at her.

Shouldn't she be dead?

How could there be breathable oxygen deep in the under surface caverns of Europa?

Look deep within.

She studied the creature.

She saw it look beyond her, behind her back, as if gesturing for her to turn around. And when she did, she saw: it was a cave, similar to the one she experienced back when lowering into the ice, but here, there was no ice.

It was dirt, and rock, and there were trees, somehow growing deep beneath the surface of the ice moon.

And there was light.

Shining through the trees.

Emanating towards her, towards that tiny, isolated beach somewhere deep within the sphere.

She finished removing her space suit, still amazed that she could breathe in this cavern. Once her suit was off, she stood in the light clothes that, when she had first put them on, the small white t-shirt and shorts, seemed like a lifetime ago, back on Vega One.

But it was warm in the cavern.

And the air was breathable.

There was no need for artificial protection.

She turned around and looked at the sea creature, patiently waiting and watching at the water's edge.

Fall forward.

She removed her boots as water spilled from them. She tossed them aside and removed her socks, tossing them across the sand.

The sand felt so soft, so warm, wet and inviting. She hadn't felt anything like that since she was a child.

And then she took a step forward.

The brilliant green leaves in the trees blew with an unseen and unexplained wind. And as she walked towards the brilliant light, the light that filtered through the trees, her thoughts were permeated with all that she could remember.

Flashes coursed through her mind; and it wasn't just recent memories of the Vegans, or of Winston, or of Jeremiah or Eli; it wasn't even memories of Sector B, back on Earth, all of which had encompassed her most recent memories as a human being.

They were those well before the others; of when she was a little girl, looking up at her smiling parents; of a little girl looking up towards the stars and the planets and admiring the heavens.

Take a leap of faith.

She opened her eyes and saw the rustling of the leaves; could this be the portal to Vega? Is this what Copernicus had spoken of? Were the trees somehow "spilling out" of a new world?

So many questions remained with her, and new questions formed. She looked back one last time. She saw the dark patch in the water; the sea creature was watching over her, waiting. And she saw her space suit lying on the beach in a pile. No need for that where she was headed, right?

But she didn't really *know*, did she?

She took a step forward.

And all will fall into place.

i

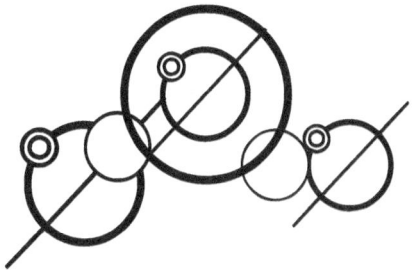

MOSES HAD SAID THAT SHE HAD BEEN HEADING THERE.

Vega.

She saw a flash of his smiling face, watching her with his piercing eyes, after the pull. And the flames. She closed her eyes, and could still hear the screaming.

Make it stop! Make it stop!

Let it go, Abby.

Let it go.

She soared through darkness as lights flashed beside her. So fast. So fleeting. And then darkness once again. Was this another worm hole? Was this the portal that the Vegans believed to be?

Would she be catapulted to Vega?

But she wasn't yet given an answer.

She opened her eyes.

There was a certain infiniteness about her vision; the colorful pallet – painted with pastels and lightly colored wisps and pinwheel variations – soared ahead of her. But there was a continuation. Not only of the colors reaching towards the dark heavens, but of the creative force ahead of her.

The mystery that existed beyond her grasp was the certain feel of mystique that washed over her as she floated forward, in a determined motion, falling forward, but ever so lightly. As if fainting in slow motion.

And she kept her face towards the vast darkness of interstellar space; her eyes remained open as she saw the painted pastels stream past her; the venting of a star, the reaching of a planet; outwards into the darkness, the mystery, the cosmos.

Her movement appeared motionless; she was surrounded by tiny, white stars which blanketed her. Countless and vast, reaching beyond to the unexplored and uninitiated obscure regions of the galaxy. But she was moving; drifting; a single, solitary woman, the heavens and the cosmos soaring just on the other side of her vision palette. She didn't know how fast she was moving. Or how distant the MACA 1 was from her now.

But she did not care.

All she could do was smile, and as she closed her eyes, a single, solitary warm tear streamed down her cheek.

And through the darkness, she closed her eyes. She felt a light wind blowing across her face. But it was a gentle wind. Refreshing. The air smelled good. Breathable. She took a deep breath. Opened her eyes.

And exhaled.

She propped herself up on her elbows.

The place looked familiar, yet different.

She looked down.

She was in red sand.

The soaring color kaleidoscope faded as she heard the light howl of wind behind her. As she slowly opened her eyes, she saw the red sand. Her hair was mussed on the side of her cheek, pressed against the cold, red sand.

She eased herself up on her elbows and looked around.

The same mountains surrounded her in the red, sandy terrain.

Mars.

But no helmet.

No breathing apparatus.

She should have certainly asphyxiated by now, shouldn't she have? She took a deep breath. There was something different about this planet.

The air tasted different.

And was processed differently.

But her lungs seemed to be processing it just fine.

Mars.

It could only be.

There could be no other.

She turned around.

She peered in the distance. She could even see the same old familiar ROVER where she had last left it at the Red Outpost.

She remembered now.

But the skies were blue.

She could breathe.

Was this the Mars on which she had been, or was this a Mars of the distant past?

What had changed?

There was an atmosphere.

There was wind, but it was a light, refreshing breeze, not the ferocious winds she had encountered or remembered.

But the same ridge surrounded her as she remembered. And as she rose to her feet, she focused on the edge where the dark ridge met the sandy surface; she saw the three mounds – the three graves in the distance next to the ridge.

She moved forward, never taking her eyes off them. And as she got closer, light shined in her eyes, causing her to stop for a moment, cover her eyes with her forearms, and lean forward. She panted, trying to catch her breath.

After a moment, she looked back up.

The light continued to shine towards her, like someone holding a mirror up to the sun and reflecting a vast beam.

Discover the key...

A voice rang in her head.

It wasn't Copernicus.

Or even Moses.

Someone was speaking to her, penetrating her mind as she moved closer.

Discover the key...

She stopped at the base of the mountain just in front of the three mounds. They were rectangular; they definitely looked to be graves. They were just the right size.

"Is this where you are? Is this where you have been?"

She caught herself for a moment. Her voice sounded different; in this vastly different version of her past.

"Who is speaking to me?"

Discover the key.

She stared intently at the middle grave. The mound of dirt looked exactly as it had when she had been there before – perhaps at least fifty years previous – and it hadn't looked like anything had changed.

But she could not get the thoughts out of her head.

She turned around and saw the light pouring out from the side of the mountain.

She dropped to her knees in front of the center grave, cupped her hand, and pushed some of the dirt to the side. And then she took some more dirt and pushed it to the side, until she tore the dirt away in a frenzy, again and again, flinging dirt with her hands, over her shoulder; as the hole formed, deeper and deeper, she dug. The soil was loose and sandy, easy to move with her hands, but what after seemed like hours, she felt the familiarity of a space suit.

She worked with intensity, leaning forward, brushing the dirt off.

She reached the visor, cleared off the sand and gasped as she saw a skull.

A space suit full of bones.

But Jeremiah's suit was lying just a mere few yards away at the base of the mountain. So where was he?

She brushed more dirt and sand off of the suit and uncovered a triangle made of stone – or rock – held by the corpse. Bones that were once fingers still gripped it after so many years; and, perhaps, it had been lying here in this grave for many years or even decades before she, Jeremiah, Winston and Eli had ever arrived on the Martian surface.

She tugged at the finger bone and pulled it away. They fell apart but she lifted the triangle up and examined it. It was dark, appeared to be carved from rock, and much heavier than it looked.

The voice rang in her head again.

Discover the key...

She turned around and rose to her feet. She walked along the edge of the mountain towards the light that fought its way out from the side of the rock, closer, and closer, until she was standing in the light.

It blinded her, but only for a moment.

For then she saw; an indentation, and as she lifted the stone triangle up towards it, the light swelled; it grew, it intensified, but it did not blind her. For in it, she felt deep love, and warmth, and saw many people, but they were concealed by the light, and the mist.

Their identities were not physically certain; but she felt a warm familiarity. For the light was not blinding. It was not foreign.

There were the planets.

The many Earth like spheres that might harbor life.

And those she knew.

Those floating globes of rock, which orbited the shining stars. But she didn't remember the one planet that she wished she had. For she remembered the water and the waves, the sand and the beaches. The mud between her toes, the blue reflection of the water and the sun.

She felt a tear stream down her cheek.

There were the soaring plumes of pastel colored gases; reaching for light years and beyond; rising through the billions of years in the past, where there had been all that had surrounded her, before there had been life.

She looked at the swirling, white hot sphere: "But you said you didn't want me to come…"

She waited for an answer.

You will always be invited to come. But the choice will always remain with you.

She turned around.

A dark, vast sea of stars remained.

"Are you really what you are? Are you the wandering star?"

And had there still been life?

Had the life remained with the planets? On the watery shores of Earth? Or underneath the rolling hilltops of Mars? Underneath the layer of ice on Europa?

Listen to me.

She watched the star as it levitated in front of her. She saw plumes of light dance from its surface, reaching towards the darkness of interstellar space.

"You!" she said. "You are the wandering star…"

Close your eyes and listen to me.

As she closed her eyes, her mind flooded with the image of an ocean. There was a vast ocean; water extended farther than her mind's eye could see.

She stood on the muddy beach, surrounded by brilliant green tropical foliage. But the sand had been finite; and then after the rising of the trees, they boarded stars and space. Had she left? For she felt she had not returned.

And then she heard a familiar voice.

It was male, reassuring.

"This is not Earth, is it? Is this your vision of what Earth should be? A painting of your own special pallet?"

And then a face appeared in the star. Smiling down on her. Different, unseen before, yet familiar and friendly. The eyes looked down on her, as if waiting for her answer.

"You," the star said. "It's always been you. You have always been special. You are unique. There is absolutely no one else in the entire vastness of interstellar space who is quite like...*you*."

She gasped.

She saw the familiarity in the face. Unparticular yet acquainted.

There was a warm smile, a certain temperament that she had come to know. A sense of familiarity; and although the star was just a star, a star that served as a guiding beacon, his face had been different.

She saw the face of her father flash through her mind, if only for an instant. She watched him approaching from the bright sunlight; the memory of his approach flooded her mind like a wave, a memory of watching him, through the window, waiting to receive him watching her.

Of smashing her palm against the control panel. And rushing out to his collapsed body with the medical team. Of performing CPR and placing him on a gurney and carrying him to emergency.

"I remember…" she said.

"And then," he said. "You must open your mind, Abagail. You must let go of your past. Of what you cling to and desperately try to remember. For you must look towards the future; towards new life and new worlds…"

He smiled down at her. "Fall forward, dear Abby. Trust. Take a leap of faith, and all will fall into place."

But the choice will always remain with you.

She floated towards the star.

It's always been you, Abagail.

Her eyes clouded with tears as the swirling, white hot sphere enlarged in her view. She closed her eyes as the tears streamed down her face, and as she got closer and closer to the star, the vast darkness of space was swallowed in a bright, and brilliant, white light, warmth and love.

You have always been special.

And when her eyes opened but saw nothing but the blue sphere; was it the same blue marble as they had called it at one time? Was it the same?

How much time had passed?

Could she remember? Did she still exist? Did the blue planet, the sphere of life, which orbited precisely 93 million miles from the sun, still exist?

Had she ever left?

For Song

5.7.17 | 10:43pm | Second Run

Thank you for reading The Europa Effect.

Please leave a review with your thoughts on either Amazon, Barnes and Noble, or Goodreads. Independently Published Authors, like myself, count on honest reviews as a means of giving our books visibility. The reviews also give authors feedback about a particular story. About elements of a story that readers connected with – or didn't. Reviews help us write better stories in the future. For you, the readers.

Thank you for being a part of sharing this book with the world.

MORE STORIES IN THE VEGA CHRONICLES

THE WANDERING STAR

THE VEGA CHRONICLES

A.L. MENGEL

MANY OF THOSE who remained living on the planet Earth could still remember the days when the oceans shifted towards the poles; and when the sea levels rose, higher, seemingly before their eyes, but certainly within a generation.

For the citizens of the planet, their memory of the water shifting was real and recent; and even years and decades later, many would recall the *Great Shift*. It became dinner table talk, bedtime stories. Those who were too young to remember the period of the *Great Shift* were told of the days when the wave came.

In those days, it was when the mass exodus from the Northern states was plastered over every news channel; every blog; throughout the internet and on every street corner. In the years during which the shift took place, and as the rotation of the planet slowed, the coastal population was forced to relocate to inland cities. Those in the Northern Hemisphere (and equally so in the Southern Hemisphere) would relocate a short distance from their previous coastal residence, and then, several years later, would be forced to move once again, as the sea crept closer…and closer…to the population.

As the planet slowed even further, and it became inevitable for those located nearest to the poles that their cities were slowly being inundated and swallowed by the Earth's waters, it came to a point that entire countries had to be abandoned as great cities were reclaimed by mother nature.

The people of the planet recalled watching in horror as the waters retreated from the tropical zones and spilled towards the north. It wasn't until the northern cities were completely swallowed, and each metropolis would fall into memory and would lie beneath vast depths of seawater, that the inhabitants of the remaining dry areas towards the equator felt the twinge of uncertainty.

Until then, when the cities were lost, it had simply been disbelief.

Some cites, like Atlanta or Rome, with a more southerly location, were not spared entirely from the assault of the waters, but the skyscrapers, and some crests on taller buildings rose from the sea. Those cities were partially inundated and still abandoned. Others, closer to the poles, were completely submerged – under a mile of water in some cases, and sentenced to decompose in a watery grave. London, New York, Toronto, and Moscow – all were lost. Santiago, Sydney, Cape Town…all underwater.

Forever.

The cities closest to the equator were also not spared.

For there, where there had once been oceans, now faded away to new, vast swaths of land as new arid deserts were born on a massive super-continent which reached around the center of the planet, spanning the equator. Once tropical zones, the land was no longer fertile; nor was it habitable. It was a harsh, sandy landscape with a blistering, relentless sun. The failing troposphere caused increasing radiation levels in these areas during sunlight; the levels lowered during darkness.

The super-continent was devoid of water, for the seas which had once surrounded cities like Havana and Mumbai, had flowed towards the poles. Areas that had once had healthy water tables experienced extreme dry conditions; muddy swamps became sandy deserts as the face of the land changed as the ocean retreated.

The phenomenon, which created new inland cities, once coastal communities, blessed with sea breezes, now were landlocked, dry and hot, many miles from the nearest water; and the air, which had thinned tremendously in the center regions of the planet, became unbreathable as the atmospheric layer of gases, which once blanketed the planet, faded. For the sun – once a harbinger of warmth and sustenance – shined at such a ferocity as to cook any mammal or reptile, and serve as a catalyst for radiation from a dying sun heading towards supernova.

Millions perished around the world, either by drowning, asphyxiation or starvation. There were some that heeded the apocalyptic warnings.

Many others maintained a sense of complacency.

The newscasts barked almost constantly about the impending doom, but until the water spilled over the shores of the coasts, and until the radiation had been felt and measured through a decomposing atmosphere, the people of the planet ignored the problem.

Until the problem became insurmountable.

It was not a cinematic horror like on the film medium; people did not tear into the streets and burn up in the sun; their skin did not boil, or slither off of their bones, nor burn and char. But the population was forced to abandon the cities closest to the equator and develop cities beneath the surface of the planet.

But there were some that ignored the warnings; their stubbornness against the reports and subsequent denial served as a catalyst for their demise – and on one particular day, the ocean rose dramatically in a very short period of time. The surge came forth like that of a cataclysmic hurricane; a giant wave was spotted in the ocean, speeding towards the coasts of the world, flowing towards the north and south poles, threatening to flatten any remaining infrastructure; for the rotation of the planet had slowed to a point that it had nearly stopped.

The wave only gave enough warning for the newscasts to break the news – *World's Coastlines Inundated* – and shortly after that, the deed had been done.

Millions drowned who didn't heed the warnings; the warnings of the event were many, and provided over the course of decades, if not longer. Scientists insisted that the slowing of the Earth's rotation could *very well possibly* reach a point where it would slow significantly in a short amount of time, creating massive tsunamis throughout the planet as the oceans displaced.

Man knew that this cataclysmic event was on the horizon, yet it was not understood.

Many could recognize the signs, over the years, indicating that the event was already in progress. But man – as an entirety – did not understand the cause behind the sudden acceleration, whether it was a slow build to a dramatic crescendo, or a sudden, unprecedented cataclysm of change; no matter who commented on the events, whether it be the slow transition or the sudden shift, it did not matter who it was, whether it was those who had been educated their entire lives on the topic, or which stellar University he or she had attended, or how specific a Degree; or how many decades of research they had performed no matter how generalized or specific. It was beyond scientific explanation and reach of man.

No one knew *why* the change in the planet was taking place, nor did they understand the direct cause of the shift of the oceans. Many who populated the planet during the years of the *Great Shift* had been studying it (or at least witnessing it) their entire lives, and the generation before them had already witnessed changes in the coastlines – beaches closer towards the poles were getting smaller, while those near the equator were enlarging. But as one generation passed the torch to the new, the problem remained: Had the Earth been truly slowing its rotation? And what was causing it to happen?

The Wandering Star is available on Amazon, Barnes and Noble, Books-A-Million and other sellers worldwide.